Books by JON GODDEN

Books by J O N G O D D E N

THE SEVEN ISLANDS
1956

THE CITY AND THE WAVE
1954

THE PEACOCK
1950

THE HOUSE BY THE SEA
1948

THE BIRD ESCAPED
1947

THE SEVEN ISLANDS

THE SEVEN ISLANDS

JON GODDEN 1906-

1956

ALFRED A. KNOPF/NEW YORK

L.C. catalog card number: 56-5770
© Jon Godden, 1956

🦌 *This is a* BORZOI BOOK *published by* ALFRED A. KNOPF, INC.

Manufactured in the United States of America.

PUBLISHED JULY 23, 1956
SECOND PRINTING, AUGUST 1956

FOR MARGARET

꠸꠸ *My grateful thanks to Mrs. Padmini Sen Gupta for reading the* MS. *of this book and to Dr. Sudhin Chose for all he did to advise and help me, especially over details of Hindu mythology.*

JON GODDEN

 *Part One*

Part One

I

In the River Ganges, above one of the many small towns and river ports with steamer ghāts and coaling-stations and fishing-boats along the shore, is a group of seven rocky islands.

There are many islands in the length of the great river between the mountains and the sea and all of them are holy ground, which is not surprising as they are surrounded by the most sacred water in all India. To bathe in the stream of the Goddess Ganga, the gentle but all-powerful Goddess, is to be cleansed of sin and worshippers carry home the holy water for eternal blessing. The dying are brought to her banks to breathe their last and bodies are cremated by the river side and the ashes consigned to her depths. The water, springing from the glaciers and snows of the Himalayas, is divine and medicinal and cures many ills, and the river is said to contain not only crocodiles and porpoises and enormous fish but gold dust and pearls. A few of these river islands are so covered with buildings, temples, monasteries, libraries of sacred books, flights of stone or marble steps, courtyards linked by covered corridors, that there is nothing of the original island to be seen except a rocky base above the stream. Others are given over to the jungle, which hides ruins of ancient temples. Some are mere clusters of boulders dividing the current, but even these will hold a Sunnyasi's cave or support the flimsy shrine of some holy man, and the boulders will be carved with sacred words and symbols.

It is not only in India that islands have drawn the religious to them. All over the world, in river, lake, and sea, lonely hermits and whole communities of monks and nuns have made of them safe roosting-places, finding holiness easier, perhaps, with a spread of water, salt or fresh, between them and the distractions of the world. The group of islands in the Ganges, sometimes called by the fishermen the blue islands, although it has other names, is remarkable because of the colour of the rocks which at times, and often in the evenings, shine as if reflecting an unnatural lapis-lazuli sky; its seven islands lie close together, a chain

4

of islands, sudden and surprising on the pale, shining breadth of the river.

The chain is, perhaps, like a water-snake swimming downstream with its head lifted above the river. The larger islands rise abruptly out of deep water where the main channel runs while, strung out behind them along the curve of the river, the rest grow smaller and more barren until the last is only a large rock which, when the river runs high, is awash and often invisible. Although none covers more than two acres of the river bed, the three main islands are roughly circular, and each has a base of piled-up boulders, rounded and polished by the current, and a crown of dark, rich vegetation, trees, bushes, creepers, growing closely and profusely; at a first glance, from the deck of a passing river steamer or from a slow-moving country-boat, the larger islands look much the same, but each in character is entirely different.

On the first, approaching from downstream, at the time of this story, was a half-ruined temple hidden in the trees and inhabited only by a holy man, a Sadhu, famous in the country round. He was reputed to have lived there for thirty years without once crossing to the mainland and to subsist on a handful of parched grain a day. The next island, which was nearest to the mainland and the largest and highest, was noted for the size of the boulders which formed its verge; the greatest of these rose from the river and the beach opposite the Sadhu's island like the back of

5

a turtle, and was known by the fishermen as the turtle's rock. The centre of this island rose to a bare hill which stuck up above the trees and in the rock face of this hill, near the summit, was the dark entrance to a cave. Here another holy man, a Fakir, had come after a lifetime as a travelling mendicant to pass his last years in solitary peace and to die, causing a great deal of trouble as, when it was known that he was no more, his remains had to be brought down the rusting iron ladder, which was the only way to reach the cave, before they could be decently disposed of on the beach below. Since then the island had been left to itself until one day in October when it suddenly became populated again and busy and noisy.

On the third island, which lay a little apart from the other two, there was nothing human at all.

2

The rains for that year were over. It was early October and the river was beginning to fall. The skies were high and cloudless and pale. The mornings and evenings were touched with coolness. The wild duck had returned.

Before the sun rose, the Sadhu descended the flight of steps that led from the temple to the beach, a small half-moon of white sand between the rocks. Unlike many of the holy men of the East, the Sadhus and Fakirs and wandering Sunnyasis, whose tangled, knotted filthy hair and naked bodies smeared with wood ash are often revolting, this man was pleasing to the eye. It was impossible to guess his age; he seemed not young but of no age. When alone he went always and in all weathers completely naked, but when he was receiving visitors, he would put on a small piece of red silk hanging from a cord round his waist to cover his genitals. No one knew his name, or if he had one. For as long as anyone could remember he had been called simply the Sadhu, although sometimes he was addressed by the few who might consider themselves his intimates as Bapuji, which means, affectionately, Little Father.

He was short and slight but there was nothing of the obvious ascetic, the lean boniness of the fanatic, nor of the soft flesh and pot belly of the well-fed religious, about his body, which,

7

in spite of his diet or because of it, radiated well-being. Under the hairless almost black skin, which shone as if oiled and polished, the muscles were well developed. His long hair, which was blue-black, clean, and shining too, hung down his back nearly to his waist. His face was broad and short, his teeth white, and his smile, like his voice, was gentle, sweet, and gay, and a little deprecating. He seldom looked directly at any of his visitors, preferring to look sideways at the ground or past them at the river. Perhaps this was because he knew that in his eyes was something wild and strange that might disturb them.

The dawn mists were rising from the surface of the river as he entered the water. He immersed himself completely three times and then stood with his hair dripping down his back while he chanted the first devotions. His voice was carried down the river with the current but there was no one to hear except the night heron perched on the rocks above him. He and the bird had the grey, damp, early-morning world to themselves.

The river below the islands was over a mile broad. From the level of the water neither bank could be seen, but a feather or two of smoke curling on the still air marked where the town lay beneath the horizon. A porpoise, somersaulting lazily close in, showed its grey back in the slack water beyond the beach. The Sadhu disappeared, leaving only a few ripples on the surface. A few moments later the porpoise showed again, but now beside him was a black head and a flash of dark shoulders which dived when he dived and rose with him in riverine play. At the edge of the slack water, where the dividing current met again, the swimmers parted and the man returned, forcing his way upstream with powerful strokes. As he neared the beach, he turned on his back and thrashed the water with his arms and legs. The sound of his laughter sent the heron up from the rocks to circle once and settle again.

The mist had gone from the river and the sky immediately overhead was blue. The sun was about to rise. The Sadhu left the water and climbed quickly over the rocks to the steps. He passed close to the heron, which did not move, and, bending down, lightly touched the dark-grey feathered back. The bird stretched its neck to look up at him and then settled again into its hunched pose.

As the man reached the top of the steps and turned to face the river, the sun lifted above the horizon, flooding river and sky with light. He flung both arms above his head in salutation and then vanished into the courtyard behind him.

On the river the black crescent shape of a boat appeared, making for the island. This was the boat of Govind, a fisherman, who was the Sadhu's main contact with the shore. Every day Govind came to the island, bringing a pitcher of milk, a little fresh fruit, and, once a week, a small bag of grain.

9

3

The courtyard of the temple was a sandy, carefully swept space, the only flat piece of ground on the island. A low balustrade protected a forty-foot drop down the rocks to the river and in the courtyard was a small thatched hut; here the Sadhu's disciples lived, although they were never allowed to stay on the island after sundown. These disciples came and went, one at a time, becoming rarer through the years and lasting a shorter time, although he did nothing positive to discourage them. The hut had been empty for over a year but a brass pitcher and two plates, left behind by the last departing one, still stood on the earth floor. Across the tree-shaded courtyard, the temple filled all the space between high, jumbled rock walls crowned with trees; to reach the rest of the island it was necessary to pass through its rooms. Against the outer wall, facing the courtyard, a shelter of dried palm leaves had been raised on bamboo poles from which hung orchids and ferns growing in pots and tins; the Sadhu watered and tended these offerings from the mainland every day, as he did the two bushes of small pale-pink roses which grew in the courtyard and the few straggling marigolds planted there, although the island possessed a wealth of flowering trees and bushes, bird-sown or wind-sown, bēl, hibiscus, cassia, champa, and other sweet-scented things.

At night the Sadhu was entirely alone except for the squirrels, birds, and snakes which shared the island with him, but in the day he often had human company. Many people from the scattered villages round, from the small town downriver, and even from further away, found it worth their while to row, or to get themselves rowed, across the wide stretch of water for the sake of sitting near him and listening to what he had to say. Among the ruins of the temple were several small, dark rooms, still habitable, although their walls were cracked and stained with age and damp. The first of these he had made into a shrine where anyone could come to pray or meditate or rest in the cool dimness; here was no image or symbol; the shrine was empty except for a large, flat, central altar stone, on which flowers and offerings were sometimes laid. The Sadhu's teaching, if it were teaching, was unorthodox; but men of many creeds and of many castes and no caste came to him and went away soothed and refreshed.

He always received his visitors at the top of the steps and it was there that he talked to them, with the river spreading away below him until it met the sky. If he were busy about his own or the island's affairs or in no mood to see them, the visitors would find the courtyard and temple empty and they would go quietly away and come back another time. No one ever penetrated beyond the temple unless, as happened very rarely, they were asked to do so; it was as if an invisible barrier lay between them and the rest of the island. With Govind the Sadhu did not stand on ceremony. When the old man climbed the steps he found the Sadhu sweeping the courtyard with a bunch of twigs, a humble task which he did twice a day when there was no disciple in residence to do it for him.

The fisherman, whose dark skin was wrinkled and knotted with age and poverty, put his basket on the ground and then knelt down to touch the holy man's feet. His bowed head was covered with close-cut grey hair. He wore only a white cloth tied round his waist and looped between his legs. The Sadhu put his broom away and the two sat down cross-legged in the thin shade.

As sometimes happened, they had not seen each other for several days, and it was obvious that Govind had something of more importance to tell of that morning than the usual small doings of his village. He gesticulated excitedly, pointing over the temple in the direction of the other islands. As the Sadhu listened, his smile disappeared. When the fisherman stopped speaking, silence fell on the courtyard which was broken only by the chattering of birds from the trees and the sound of the river. The two men sat facing each other, Govind fidgeting and picking at his toes, the Sadhu immobile, his eyes half shut. Suddenly he stood up, rising with one quick, graceful movement, walked to the basket and, taking out the bag of grain, the fruit, and the pitcher of milk, vanished into the temple.

The fisherman waited where he was until the empty brass

vessel appeared in the doorway of the main room, put there apparently by an invisible hand. This he took as a signal of dismissal and, placing the pitcher under its cloth, prostrated himself before the temple, picked up his basket, and departed down the steps.

When he had gone, the Sadhu reappeared and standing by the balustrade watched the boat out of sight. There was no other movement on the river or sign of life. He was carrying the bag of grain and now he walked into the centre of the courtyard. At once the air was thick with wings that beat about him as he scattered the corn. The courtyard was full of birds, mynahs and sparrows and the island's pair of doves; they perched on his shoulders and outstretched arm and even on his head before descending to the ground. A few crows appeared and an egret alighted on the balustrade to watch the feast. As the Sadhu slowly ate a handful of the parched grain, grinding each particle between his teeth, his face was as serene as it had been before the fisherman told his story. Tying up the neck of the cotton bag, he walked between the birds back to the temple. If the news that he had heard still distressed him he gave no sign but went about his daily ritual as he always did, taking his time.

The interior of the temple was dark and cool. The thick walls were alcoved and the several small rooms and dark passages led out of each other. Close to the central shrine and reached by a narrow entrance through which a man could just squeeze was a small cell; this was built between two large boulders that leant out over the river and was only big enough to hold one human being in a crouching position. In the floor was a hole over the river and in the outer wall was a loophole, a slit for light and air. Visitors to the temple would peer into this cell with awed faces, but it was a long time since the Sadhu had crouched there in mortification of the body or in meditation. Long ago he had passed into a spiritual region where such practices were no longer necessary.

Now he went quietly about the temple rooms in the green light that came as much from the river as from the trees. He swept the floors and dusted the altar stone and put fresh flowers there; this he did slowly and smoothly, as if he were following the pattern of a ritual temple dance performed to an inner rhythm of his own. When all was as it should be in the temple, he took his pitcher of milk and two earthenware saucers from an alcove, and following a passage and climbing a short flight of steps, emerged into the sunshine.

Behind the temple was an open space from which a maze of narrow sandy paths wound between the rocks and trunks of trees, in and out and round, crossing and recrossing each other, sometimes broadening into small recesses or rock chambers, often tree-shadowed with glimpses between the rocks of the river below. These paths were bordered with flowering bushes and in some places cut into rough steps which led up and down, but all at last ended on the bare rock ledges and huge boulders which confronted the other islands.

The Sadhu followed a path that led to an inner chamber deep among the rocks. This was the secret centre of the island, its navel, hidden by rock walls from everything except the sky. On one side a fig tree, a pipal, sprang, as such trees do, apparently from the rock itself. Here he set the saucers down, one among the tree roots and the other on a higher ledge in the rocks, and filled them with milk. The milk which Govind ferried across the water was not for the Sadhu but for his snakes.

No one, not even his disciples, knew how the Sadhu spent his time when he was not at his devotions or conversing with his visitors at the top of the stone steps. Sometimes a fisherman would surprise him bathing in the lee of the island, diving and tumbling like an otter, or see him, with a striped squirrel on his shoulder, sitting cross-legged on the rocks below the temple stringing flower-heads into long chains. In the evenings he was often seen from the river steamers and country-boats, perched on his favourite high rock ledge which jutted out over the river. Here he would sit facing the sunset, his long hair lifting in the breeze. The sound of his singing and chanting would be carried far down the river long after darkness had fallen and the stars had appeared. But no living thing, unless it were a snake or a dozing bird, knew where or how he spent his nights.

Many strange and wonderful tales were told of him in the

villages and countryside. It was said that he could walk on the water when he felt like it, and pass in this manner from island to island and even visit the mainland at will. It was hinted that he could fly, or, if not exactly fly as a bird does, raise himself from the ground to the height of a small tree. He was reputed to have tamed every snake and bird on the island and to converse with them as other men do with men. This last rumour, as rumours generally are, was partly true.

He stood waiting with the pitcher in his hand until he heard a dry rustling and slithering and saw something moving in the dead leaves between the rocks. Then he went quietly away, knowing that, although his presence would not deter them, the snakes preferred to drink unobserved, especially when the sun was shining. He returned to the temple and put the pitcher in a cool place close to his other few possessions.

Like ordinary men he had his own little arrangements for living but these were of the simplest. A cotton bag of grain hanging from a nail in the wall, his lota, a jar of cold water, a bottle of oil for his body and hair, a comb, a few coins which were offerings tied in a cloth for the purchase of these necessities when they were not given. He had a particular and hidden spot where he relieved himself and all could be carried away by the all-receiving river, and also several warm sandy lairs about the island where he could curl up and doze, and favourite smooth rocks where he could stretch himself out in the sun.

He now sought one of these rocks and lay down on his back
with his arms folded under his head. The rock was pleasantly
warm and smooth under him. The sun beat down on his naked
body from a clear blue sky. He lay so still that presently a column
of ants, intent on their own affairs, marched across his thighs.
He felt the myriad small moving legs on his skin and waited
patiently without flexing a muscle or twitching his skin until
the column had passed, before turning over and presenting
his back to the sun.

He was never alone on the island for long, and now a small
squirrel, or chipmunk, whose light-grey back was striped with
brown, joined him and sat chattering and flicking its tail beside
him. He stroked it gently, as the God Rama once had done and
left the mark of his divine fingers for ever on soft squirrel fur.
When it scampered away to the trees, a lizard appeared on the
rock close to his head. There were many lizards on the island,
including a solitary iguana, or giant monitor, which inhabited
the steep rocks facing the mainland and was seldom seen even
by him. The Sadhu lifted his head from his arms and looked
into the small, glass-bright, lizard eyes; he could see the pulse
beating in the yellow-white throat and presently he moved
his hand towards it and touched the creature's scaly back. The
sun, mounting higher, beat down on the rock and a delicate
film of steam arose from the man's now glistening body. The
shadows of the trees shortened behind him and the sky paled.

Something passing and repassing between the sun and the rock roused him. As he sat up, the lizard vanished and the shadow came again, sweeping over the rocks. He looked up into the sky.

The great grey-headed fishing eagle sailed in close above the trees. He could feel the rush of air displaced by the dark wings and see the pale head turned down to watch him. High in the sky its mate circled too above the island. Never before had the eagles come to him; he had always gone to them, knowing that eagles and snakes, fabulous and sacred as both are to Hindus, are ancient enemies best kept apart. At this time of year the birds should have been thinking of nesting, and, remembering what Govind had told him that morning, the Sadhu knew what had disturbed them. He stood up and called to them their own sad and raucous cry. The eagle passed close over him once again and then spiralled up in widening circles to join its mate. He stood for a few moments longer on the rocks and watched the two specks wheeling against the blue. He had only half believed the fisherman's story but now the eagles confirmed it. The time had come when he must go and see for himself.

Anyone following the secret paths behind the temple would emerge out of the trees above the rock ledges and be plainly seen from the other islands. The Sadhu at this stage had no intention of showing himself and when he left the rocks he followed the narrow gully that led down to the river. Skirting the boulders, sometimes lowering himself into the stream and keeping himself from being swept away in the fierce current by hanging on to the tough trailing creepers that hung down to the water from the trees, he worked his way slowly round the island until he reached a point where, standing up to his waist in the river in the cleft between two boulders, he could see without being seen. From here the islands looked as if they were linked together by their green reflections in the water.

The eagles were now circling over the third island in the chain, whose screen of trees came down to the water's edge, but the nearer island was transformed. It was as busy and as agitated as a disturbed ant-hill.

Men were everywhere. They perched on the rocks and swarmed on the beaches and stood about in knots and clusters. Two country-boats laden with still more men were approaching the island. A barge piled high with bricks was being unloaded on the shore. Sheets of corrugated-iron were carried across the rocks and stacked at the foot of the hill. Men were digging between the rocks and slashing at the undergrowth with knives that shone in the sunlight. To the Sadhu it seemed incredible that so much could have been done in a few days and such a change have come over this island while he was busy with his own affairs. As he watched, a tree toppled and fell. The sound of its fall came across the water to him above the shouts and cries and the creaking of oars. He looked towards the bird island where a cloud of egrets rose up from the trees and settled again and his face darkened.

The Sadhu's eyes were as long-sighted and as clear as a bird's and he saw every detail of the scene across the water, but he did not understand all he saw. Among the half-naked coolies and workmen was a small party of men dressed in white muslin, one of whom, a tall old man with thick white hair, strode excitedly from place to place waving his arms and pointing. He was followed closely by a shorter man carrying a roll of papers under his arm. The Sadhu guessed that these were the ringleaders, the men in charge; but he could make nothing of the strange machine, a concrete-mixer, now being unloaded on the beach and when a large notice-board was set up at the edge of the water he could not read the letters on it. He watched a group of small distant figures raise a flagstaff among the rocks on top of the hill, but the tricolour flag which presently waved from it meant nothing to him. He was staring at this disturbing and unnatural spot of colour in perplexity when a boat came into view from behind the island, propelled by a rower in the bows and by a steersman standing upright with a large paddle in the stern. In the centre was a small cabin or shelter made of bamboo and plaited wickerwork, on the roof of which sat a fat man with his legs drawn up under him. He was dressed in a dhotie and a brown coat buttoned up to the chin and a round black hat. As the Sadhu watched the boat draw in to the bank and the man climb ashore and approach the white-clad group, his face cleared. Hari Das Thirani, the rich merchant and man of the world, was also a searcher after the truth and his pupil and friend. Today was the day for his weekly visit to the Sadhu's island. By that evening the meaning of this invasion of the islands would be made clear and the gaps in the ignorant Govind's story be filled.

The Sadhu left the river and climbed over the rocks to the trees, no longer troubling to conceal himself. The new inhabitants of the island across the water were too busy to concern themselves with him. Only the eagles saw him go.

4

That afternoon an unusually large number of visitors, perhaps as many as twenty-five, came to see the Sadhu. He had known that they would come and he was ready for them. He had the power, when he chose to use it, of seeing some way into the future, and he also knew his parishioners. He had known that as soon as possible they would seize the chance of satisfying their curiosity as to what was happening on the other island and of fulfilling a spiritual need at the same time and for the same boat hire. He had eaten his meal of fresh fruit punctually at midday, bathed again and oiled himself and donned his strip of poppy-coloured silk. When the first boat drew in to the beach he was seated cross-legged at the top of the stone steps with a small heap of the pale roses beside him.

All that afternoon he sat there while the people came and went. To some he said a few words or only acknowledged their greeting as they passed close by him on their way to the temple. Others squatted down beside him and with them he talked, or listened, with eyes half closed and head held back, to all they had to say. To many he handed a rose as they left, placing it between their cupped palms and receiving a coin which they placed on the step beside him as an offering. It was a gay and careless scene with nothing solemn or formal about it. Those who had shoes shuffled them off and left them with the row of other shoes inside the courtyard. A party of young men joked together as they climbed the steps; one wore a shirt whose vivid heliotrope shone against the trees and was reflected in the water below. A family party picnicked on the beach after a visit to the temple, the women bunched together on the rocks, the children, shedding what clothes they wore, splashing and tumbling and shouting in the shallow water with more than their usual abandon, as if they knew that here, if anywhere, they could give free rein to their animal spirits. The sun began its evening slant towards the river. The colours slowly changed and deepened. The boats, one by one, put off from the beach, leaving only the marks of their prows on the sand. When Hari Das Thirani climbed the steps, using his stick with the chased silver handle and carrying his important stomach well before him, nearly everyone had gone. Only a humble black shell of a boat shared the beach with his. Temple and courtyard were empty. The row of shoes had disappeared. Only one man still waited at the top of the steps and on the Sadhu's lap, held in his arms, was a naked sleeping child.

This child, Prem, a pet of the Sadhu, was a lively, gay, small creature of whom he was very fond. Prem had black curls, a sharp, clever, merry face and small bright eyes and a light bird-like body with thin legs and arms. His father, Ram Kishen, a strong, ugly young man with bandy legs and long arms and a pock-marked, intelligent face was a Chandal, the lowest of the low among the Untouchables, an outcaste who worked at the burning ghāts below the town, plunging into the river to sink the half-burnt corpses of the poor. The lot of the Untouchables —renamed Harijans, Sons of God, by Ghandiji—is now very different from what it was when to Hindus even their shadows, even the sight of them, was a pollution. Now most temples and schools and professions are open to them and they are protected by law, but even today they are scavengers and cleaners and avoided by the orthodox. Ram Kishen was an unfortunate man in more ways than one; his wife and two elder children had died of the same disease which had marked his face and this son was all that he had left. He did not accept his humble role in life patiently, as most of his kind still do, and his morose and surly temper and a certain wildness, even savageness, about him made him disliked and feared by almost everyone except the Sadhu.

He stood up as the merchant approached and his face, which had been animated and happy as he talked to the Sadhu, was now sullen and dark. He scowled and picked the child up from the holy man's lap and, holding him over his shoulder, without a word or a backward glance, clambered over the rocks to the beach, avoiding the steps.

The Sadhu watched him go and not until the boat had put off from the beach and the wail of the suddenly woken child had died away did he turn to Hari, who stood hesitating a few steps below him. Then he pointed to the place beside him where the Untouchable had sat. When the merchant hesitated even more, a look of distaste on his smooth, olive-coloured face under the red caste-mark on the forehead, the Sadhu laughed. It was a gay, mocking sound, and Hari shrugged his fat shoulders and sat down, smoothing the skirts of his coat under him.

For a few moments they sat together in silence. On the beach below them the two boatmen sat smoking, their backs turned to the steps. Beyond them and their boat the world was all water and sky. The river ran wide and glassy and colourless past the chain of islands; its shoals were wrinkled, dark patches between the sandbanks; the further shore was marked, when a breeze blew, by drifting clouds of sand. The line of blue hills along the horizon looked as insubstantial as the white clouds above them.

From the top of the steps the river port could be plainly seen; the distinct if distant outline of its few buildings and the summits of its trees pinned the narrow green line of the river bank to the sky. A steamer was waiting at the jetty below a huge pile of coal and the masts of fishing-boats stuck up along the bank. Hari lived and worked in the little town behind the port. He now sat with his shoulder turned away from it and his face to the river.

The Sadhu spoke first, which was unusual; his way was to listen and then to answer, but now he lifted his hand to compel the other man's attention and his soft, sing-song voice went on, quietly but with authority, almost as if he were a school-master giving an obstinate pupil a difficult lesson, until the merchant's uneasiness left him and he settled himself more comfortably on the stone step. Hari was a shrewd business man, whose chief interest in life was the amassing of money for money's sake. He was to all appearances a devout Jain and a good family man, but he was also a man of many contradictions: mean and generous, physically careful and mentally bold, curious and unsatisfied. Ten years ago he had first come to the island and, in his restless and secret search for what he could not name, had found the Sadhu. He now came regularly, not exactly secretly, but unostentatiously, when no one else of his kin was likely to be about. The two were now not only master and disciple, teacher and pupil, if these they had ever been, but friends.

When the lesson, if lesson it had been, was over, it was Hari's turn to speak and soon the weekly argument and discussion began. This did not last as long as it usually did. The Sadhu brought it to a close after glancing towards the descending sun. He changed his position, moving nearer to the other man, crossing one leg over his knee and putting his foot on a lower step, to indicate that they were now to leave abstruse subjects and to concern themselves with wordly things. It was he who now asked questions and the merchant who answered them.

26

Hari's answers filled in and corrected the rough sketch which Govind had given the Sadhu that morning of what was taking place on the next island and explained much that the holy man had seen with his own eyes. He learned first that the white-clad group of men whom he had watched were members of a sect of the Vaishnavas, followers of Vishnu, the second of the three aspects of the Supreme Being, the Hindu Triad, Brahma the Creator, Vishnu the Preserver, and Siva the Destroyer, and that they intended to found an ashram on the island, to build a school for the training of religious students, a hostel, a guest-house, and a temple in honour of the Lord Krishna, the most popular of the ten avatars or incarnations of Vishnu.

As he listened, the Sadhu's face darkened and he scowled, much as Ram Kishen had done, and the merchant paused in his story to ask what objections could there possibly be to what they must admit was a good and godly project. The followers of Krishna, in certain of his aspects, were regarded doubtfully by some as being devotees more of eroticism and sex-worship than of the mystic and spiritual, but Dr. Mahabir Prasad Mishra, a Doctor of Philosophy, the leader and founder of this enterprise, was an earnest, saintly, white-haired old man above such suspicion. Only that morning this Mishra had said that he did not intend his ashram to be exclusive and given over entirely to the meditative and scholarly life, but that the temple when built would welcome worshippers, rich and poor, from the

27

mainland. When the Sadhu did not answer, Hari said gently that if the holy man feared for the safety of the wild life of the islands, of the birds, whose welfare everyone knew was his special concern, he need not worry. As a Jain he, Hari, shared the Sadhu's concern, and Dr. Mishra had assured him that all life on the island would be considered sacred. Only that morning a workman had been dismissed for killing a snake which he had surprised among the rocks.

At this news the Sadhu's face lightened, and then became gloomy again. When he had learnt all that he could from Hari, including the meaning of the flag and the use of the strange machine on the beach, he was silent for some time. He nodded his head once or twice and then shook it sadly. Hari laughed and stretched himself, and the Sadhu lifted his hand once more, this time in blessing and dismissal. He accompanied his visitor down the steps to the beach and watched him embark between the two boatmen. Standing on the rocks, he saw the merchant, sitting on his folded rug on the cabin roof of the boat, his legs in their socks and slippers dangling over the side, whirl quickly away on the current towards the town.

The sun was low in the sky and the river was stained with colour. Quickly the Sadhu moved over the rocks and the beach, searching for any debris which his visitors might have left behind. The peel of an orange, a used basket made of leaves, brown ends of cigarettes, and a few twists of paper were flung

28

far out into the water. Now the only signs left to show that anyone except himself had been on the island that day were the
marks left by the boats on the sand, and these he carefully
smoothed out with his hands.

When the island was itself again, he bounded up the steps
and through the archway to reappear a few moments later without his piece of red silk. He was alone with the river and the
sky and, after long hours of sitting cross-legged on the stone,
his body found violent movement necessary. His recent visitors
would have been astonished if they could have seen him then.
He stretched himself, leapt from rock to rock, turned cart-
wheels on the sand, and finally plunged into the river, where
the gambols and cavorting went on and the water, now coloured
pink by the setting sun, was thrown up in a cloud of spray.
When he emerged and stood on the rocks again, he shook himself as any animal does after its bath and, throwing his long
hair back from his shoulders, climbed the rocks as agilely as a
monkey to his evening perch high above the river.

This rock, narrowing at its end to a point and flattened across
its top to a seating-place, jutted far out over the water towards
the sunset. On it the heads of a few marigolds were strewn
and at its extremity rags, tied to two foot-high sticks embedded
in the rock, flew like prayer flags. Here the Sadhu seated himself, crossing his legs in the lotus position.

The sun was going down, its red disk vanishing into a nest

of purple clouds. The sky was flame and green and gold, an angry sunset, but above the islands the pure blue persisted, untouched by the tide of colour. The evening breeze sent the Sadhu's long hair streaming back from his shoulders. He lifted his arms to the sky, rocked his body backwards and forwards as his high chanting and singing began. A flight of duck passed across the sunset. Far out, in the main channel, the black shape of a river steamer was making its way upstream, its funnel sharp against the yellow sky, its lights, red and gold, reflected in the shining water. The throbbing of its paddle-wheels came clearly over the river, but the Sadhu neither saw nor heard it. He had gone, leaving his body to sway and chant on the rock, and in ecstasy was speeding towards the sunset. Darkness had fallen over the island before he returned to himself.

5

It was night and in the rock chamber at the centre of the island the Sadhu was waiting for the moon to rise. He had slept for an hour or two soon after it grew dark, curled up on the sandy ledge between the roots of the pipal, but now he sat with his back against the rock and his arms clasping his knees. The small rock-enclosed space round him was a well of darkness with the starry sky for a roof.

He was not alone. The snakes, who a few hours before had come in the starlight for the milk in the refilled saucers, still kept him company. He could hear them slithering over the rocks and sandy floor and feel them near him. One drew its length across his instep as he sat and another, satiated and sleepy in its coils beside him, pressed against the warmth of his body. This, he knew, was his rat snake, whose dark scales were now silvery with age; it was the largest snake on the island, nearly ten feet long, as thick as a man's arm, and harmless, unlike the krait entwined at that moment among the tree roots near his head. The snakes of the island accepted the Sadhu, as he did them. He was careful not to make a sudden or violent movement near them and not to tread on them as they lay across the paths, as they often did in the sunlight. He provided them with milk and warmth and they in their turn kept the rat and mouse and beetle population of the island within reasonable limits. Their own numbers had greatly increased with the years. Not only did the soft white eggs hatch out from time to time, but the snakes of the other islands must have learned in some mysterious fashion of the hospitality offered to their kind by the Sadhu and have decided to brave the swim across the channels; on these islands, and more especially on the nearest, a snake of any kind was now a rarity. A few of the young ones disappeared, departing perhaps for the mainland, preferring the dangers of the journey to the rule of their· ancestors, but the Sadhu's island was becoming overcrowded. This did not worry the holy man; to welcome the newcomers and to make them feel at home, he was not above giving them a little music from time to time on the snake-charmer's pipes which he kept hidden behind the temple; then he would crouch down on a sandy patch among the rocks with the mouthpiece to his lips while the snakes gathered round as if to listen and the island's pair of cobras swayed and danced, their hoods extended against the sky.

The night was cold for the time of year. The mist that hung over the river drifted up between the rocks and the tree trunks, never rising more than a foot or so above the level of the island, but bringing with it a damp chill. When the months of true cold weather came, the Sadhu would often light a small fire of twigs and broken branches in the middle of his rock chamber and crouch over it until daylight. Now, early in the year as it was, moved perhaps by a sudden need for light and warmth which would help him illuminate his thoughts and plan his moves for the night after the moon had made her appearance, he stood up and, crossing the open space, followed the path back to the temple.

He could see in the dark almost as a wild cat does, well enough to avoid anything lying across his path. The temple was silent and dark. As he entered the low doorway, the bats which in the daytime hung head downwards from the roofs inside skimmed past his head, going and coming through the blackness of the rooms and out to the dark sky beyond. Their high twittering cries were in his ears as he bent for the bundle of dried sticks. His boxes of matches, which were brought by the fisherman, were kept in a small tin high in a niche in the wall to protect them from damp.

The fire blazed up from its nest of dead leaves and twigs. The flames made bold patterns on the darkness and painted the rock walls with their light. The Sadhu sat beside the fire, feeding it from the pile of broken sticks. The blue wood-smoke spiralled up with the flying sparks towards the stars. In the trees near by the birds stirred uneasily, woke, and shifted on their perches, complained a little, and fell asleep again, but the snakes were not alarmed. They drew nearer to the warmth, uncurling from their resting-places on the rocks, sliding nearer; their cold eyes reflected the light of the flames. Although the branches of the

33

pipal tree were illumined from below, not a chink or thread of firelight escaped to the river, but, if anyone had chanced to look down from a plane crossing high above the river, as planes often did on their journey across the continent, he might have seen a spot of flickering light on the dark emptiness of water, a ruby glow that was larger than the light of any fishing-boat.

The Sadhu sat upright and still among the snakes. He was a part of the living circle round the fire. Only his hand moved as another stick was added to the blaze. The firelight shone on the polished skin of his chest and showed the whites of his eyes. The great rat snake pressed once more against his thigh and laid its spear-shaped head across his knee. Above him the sky slowly paled and the stars disappeared, but he did not move until the moon, still almost a perfect disk, only a day or two above its fulness, rose over the rim of the rock walls. Then he rested his hands on his lap and allowed the fire to sink to a glow. After a few minutes he gently lifted the snake's head from his knee and rose cautiously to his feet.

The rock chamber was now full of a pale light in which he could make out the coiled shapes round the dying fire. Picking his way between them, he reached the path and followed it, not to the temple but over higher ground between the rocks and then steeply down between dark tree trunks to the river. Here in a narrow bay, hidden behind an enormous boulder, he kept the boat which no one, not even Ram Kishen or the most persistent of his disciples, not even the riverman Govind, had ever glimpsed or suspected.

It was a small and shallow boat, if boat it could be called, being only a hollowed-out tree trunk sharpened at the bows. Many years ago, early one morning in the rainy season, he had found it cast up on the rocks by the river, a very different river, swollen and brown, roaring past the chain of islands under low, scurrying grey clouds and carrying on its swirling muddied waters the wreckage of the rains: planks and branches, the ruins of the houses, the corpses of drowned trees and animals. Accepting the boat as a gift from the river, he had righted it and brought it carefully round the island to this hidden place. The paddle had been made by himself from the branch of a tree and was long enough to allow him, when coming downriver with the current, to stand up and use it as a steersman's oar. The boat was so low in the water, its sides only a few inches above the river, that from a distance it was invisible. Perhaps it was some fishermen, waking in their own boat in the dawn after a long night of fishing, who had started the legend of the Sadhu's ability to walk on the water as other men walk on land; they had seen the Sadhu's distant figure, upright and alone, gliding back to the island after his nocturnal wanderings. The Sadhu had never contradicted this rumour; what simple, faithful people do not know will not harm them; but he had been careful to limit his voyages to the night.

35

Now, seating himself, he undid the rope of knotted creepers and cast off from the shore, rounded the boulder, and slowly forced the boat upstream, keeping close in to the island; across the moonlit water a few lights still shone in the distant villages along the bank. Once he had reached the limits of his own shore and launched out of its black shadow into the full moonlight, he felt the fierce current and, strong as his arms were, it was all he could do to cross the channel between one island and the next; he had to paddle with all his strength to land where he wished to land, well above the notice-board which, under the moon, looked startlingly white and new. He knew now what its black letters spelt, Krishnalilashram. Near it, he now saw, a rough shelter had been made before which a lantern was burning. Hari had told him that a watchman was to be left on the island every night to guard the stock of building-materials. On the open silver water the Sadhu and his boat were black and conspicuous; it was to be hoped that the man, as is the way with watchmen, was safely asleep behind his lamp.

Avoiding the sandy bays where the mark of the prow would be seen, he wedged the boat in between the rocks in the shadow of a huge hibiscus bush whose trumpet flowers were crimson in the moonlight. The Sadhu stepped ashore and disappeared into the undergrowth. Here small trees and bushes came down to the water's edge in what had once been a garden planted by a long-forgotten religious community, of whose temple nothing now remained except its scattered stones. Marigolds persisted in the weeds beside the path; hibiscus, banana, pomegranate, guava struggled with the indigenous scrub jungle along the base of the hill whose bare summit rose above him into the silver sky. He knew this island almost as well as his own and had considered it since the old Fakir died as a part of his parish for which he was in his own way responsible. His feet soon found the narrow path which had persisted in the vegetation. Following it, he advanced cautiously, bending under the overhanging branches, making no sound. The path wound past great boulders and climbed ancient roughly made steps from level to level. The moon shone through the leaves bewilderingly and flooded the open spaces among the rocks with a clear, steady light. The scent of flowers and of leaves bruised by his passing hung on the still air.

Suddenly he came upon a newly cleared patch of ground, not much larger than a spread blanket but already dug and fenced with split bamboo. He knew from Hari that the ashram intended to grow corn, fruit, and vegetables on every available plot of ground. He also knew that after all the proposed buildings which Hari enumerated had been built—the temple, the hostel, the dharamsala or guesthouse, classrooms, and a latrine —there would not be many such plots left among the rocks, terrace the island as ingeniously as they might. The villagers of the mainland were right in believing that they would be asked to provision the place. Govind that morning had reflected their greed and elation; a community as well-to-do as this one was reported to be, financed largely by a devout, wealthy gentleman from Benares, would be sure to pay generously.

The Sadhu passed the fence and came upon a pile of bricks. The vegetation ended abruptly. He had reached the point directly facing his own island and here any trees that had flourished among the rocks had been felled, bushes torn up and an attempt made here and there to level the ground. Close to the beach was the straw roof of the watchman's hut. Between it and the Sadhu, the uneven, rocky terrain was covered with stacked bricks, raw in the moonlight, planks, a pile of corrugated-iron sheets, sacks, iron rods, and a heap of white cement powder. Cautiously he skirted the scene, viewing it from all angles and keeping as far as possible in the shadow of the rocks. From the lower slopes of the hill came a strong stench. During his conducted tour of the island that morning, Hari had been told that the latrines were to be built on the jutting point of rock where the island shelved abruptly to the river; but the workmen and coolies could not be expected to wait for them. The Sadhu, used to the lonely cleanliness of his own island, wrinkled his nose in distaste and, hastily leaving the rocks, stepped boldly out into the moonlight.

Examining everything he saw, he moved towards the beach. Sticks had been stuck into the ground to mark the sites of future buildings. Strings tied to pegs planted between the rocks showed where flights of steps would be. Spades and workmen's tools had been left piled together. He stood for some time with the moon shining down on him, a dark, glistening, incongruous figure, beside the strange shape of the concrete-mixer. He knew now what it was but it still baffled him and he touched it cautiously, as if it were an interesting animal that he had not come across before. Hari had told him that the school and guesthouse were to be on the other side of the island facing the mainland. Knowing the ground as he did, the Sadhu thought that this would be impossible. There the boulders were of immense size and the slope to the central hill too steep. He looked round and shook his head.

Hari had said that this Dr. Mishra expected over a hundred novitiates and many Vairagis eventually to join him. There was not enough room. Two hundred men or more, devout as they might be and with the best of intentions, could not live on this rock cheek by jowl, one on top of the other, like pigeons in a coop. Before long they would turn their attention to the bird island which, from their point of view, belonged to no one and was empty, quite uninhabited.

Troubled and confused by his thoughts, the Sadhu climbed down over the rocks, looking for the site of the new temple on which, as Hari had told him, an enthusiastic start had already been made. He knew that it was to rise directly from the turtle-backed boulder, the largest on the island, from which flights of steps would later lead down to the water. A flat base of brick and concrete had already been laid over the rock late that evening and covered by damp sacking so that the concrete of the floor might set slowly and not crack when the sun rose. The Sadhu, never having seen concrete before, stepped down, planting one foot in a space between the strips of sacking. He moved back hastily, disliking the damp cold touch, but not before he had left the deep print of his foot, clear and sharp in every detail, in the wet concrete. It was then, seeing the brick bases of the pillars and the piles of bricks against the rock wall behind him that marked the spot where the inner space, the place of the Gods, was to be, that he knew where he was. For a moment he was disconcerted then, as he stared down at his own imprint, his teeth showed in the moonlight in a broad smile.

Squatting down on his heels, he carefully altered the position of the sacking, moving the strips so that they covered the footprint. Next morning the masons would be prepared to swear that the mark had not been there when they covered the newly laid floor. Every villager in the neighbourhood knew that the island was haunted. Tales of bhūts and demons seen among the ruined temples had been told long before the old Fakir had died. Many of the men working on the island would have been recruited from the villages. The Sadhu knew what a web can be spun from less evidence than a footprint appearing from nowhere in the night.

As he stood up again, he looked towards the watchman's shelter. It was surprising that anyone had been found willing to stay alone all night on the island. The man must either be a stranger, or Pratap Singh, who, as everyone knew, was afraid of nothing alive or dead.

He approached the shelter silently but the sound of snoring coming from it told him that there was no need for excessive caution. He bent down to peer under the low thatch roof. A large bare foot stuck out from the blanket. No one would be able to say that this foot had made the small and slender footprint in the concrete.

It was indeed Pratap Singh, the Sikh, a big and impressive-looking man who had once been a soldier. He was a regular visitor to the Sadhu's temple and well known to him as a devout, likable, and plausible rogue. A few weeks before, he had once again lost his licence to drive the town's one and only ancient taxi-cab and since then, as the Sadhu knew, he had gone back to his second profession of watchman and had been living as best as he could. The light of the lantern shone on the black beard streaked with grey and on the long black hair fastened in the Sikh's knot on the top of the head, and on the large, fierce, hooked nose. Beside him lay his thick wooden staff.

Resisting an impulse to tweak Pratap Singh's big toe, the Sadhu withdrew. He was laughing silently. And now it seemed as if the moonlight, that seductive gold and silver flood, must have reached his brain, for he indulged in a series of childish, mischievous, small pranks. He leapt about the rocks with his long hair flying, laughing to himself silently, plunged his hands into the heap of cement, and scattered the powder over the rocks until they shone. He collected the workmen's tools and every pick and shovel and hid them under a sheet of corrugated iron. The pegs and strings marking future flights of steps were left alone, being too difficult to move, but the sticks which showed where the buildings would rise were soon transplanted to other and unsuitable sites among the rocks. As a last gesture, he knelt on the rock behind the unbuilt temple and, reaching down, dropped the heads of marigold flowers on the bricks that marked the place where the image of the God would stand.

The moon was now directly overhead. In a few hours dawn would break over the river. He had not yet paid his visit to the bird island but the mischievous active mood was still on him. Running lightly over the open rocks, he plunged into the bushes again and followed a steep short-cut that only he knew, scrambling on all fours, to the summit of the hill.

Standing by the flagstaff, he waited a few minutes to get his breath. The silvered world stretched out below him, river and sky meeting in a gauzy haze. On the shining expanse of water the curving chain of islands and their reflections were black and sharp. The tumbled rocks of his own shore were startlingly clear but his temple was hidden in the trees. He examined the flagstaff carefully, fingering the ropes; the flag was out of his reach and he did not understand the ropes and presently he lay flat on the ground at the edge of the cliff and looked down. The mouth of the deserted cave was hidden but he could see the iron ladder straddling the rock. Below him were the beach and the straw roof of the hut. Picking up a small pebble, he aimed carefully. The pebble bounced from the roof on to the stones and he followed the sound of its fall, which was astonishingly loud on the still night, by raising his head and uttering an owl's mournful cry.

Pratap Singh emerged from the hut into the moonlight, holding his staff. He looked a dignified, if slightly ridiculous, figure in his Sikh's shorts and a loose shirt, as he shaded his eyes against the moon and looked around. Nothing moved on the beach or on the rocks and there was nothing to hear. He walked a few steps this way and that, brandishing his staff and grumbling to himself. The Sadhu shook with silent laughter as he watched; then he raised his arms and cried the owl's cry once more. The man on the rocks below swung round and peered up at the hill, shrugged his shoulders, yawned, scratched himself, and sauntered back to the hut. The Sadhu knew that when questioned Pratap Singh would declare that he had spent the whole night wide awake and watchful, walking round and round the island, and that nothing had disturbed its peace except the calling of an owl. It would not matter if no one believed

him. He would stick to his story once it was told and nothing
would shake him.

Moving carefully, the Sadhu backed away from the cliff and
stood up. He made his way by another route to where he had
left his boat, stopping often to listen. He was almost certain that
Pratap Singh was by now snoring comfortably again but he
knew that it is never wise to underestimate any man; the Sikh
was, until it paid him to be otherwise, a good watchman according to his own ideas, and not only brave but honest. But
the night was undisturbed again; nothing moved among the
bushes and there was nothing to be heard except the sound of
the river as it raced through the channel between the islands.

The Sadhu got into his boat once more, pushed off, and paddled round the side of the island until it was between him and
the hut. Across the water on which the moonlight played and
danced lay the dark bulk of the bird island. He directed his
course silently towards it.

*　　*　　*

Even in the daytime the approaches to this third island of
the chain were dim, green, and mysterious; at night the shadows
were black and the silence profound. Dipping his paddle softly
in and out of the water, the Sadhu passed from the moonlight

44

into the darkness under the trees which came down to the water's edge and overhung the river. Here was another beach, another strip of sand between the rocks, but it was strewn only with fallen leaves and marked only by the tracks of water birds. The boat glided in and touched the sand without a sound. He stepped ashore and stood for a moment, listening.

The silence was unbroken but he knew that his arrival had been noted. He hesitated, as if he were waiting for permission to advance or for an invisible barrier to lift. Always, when he came to the island, he felt a cold strangeness close round him, as if the air here was of another world. This strangeness was not inimical; he knew that his presence was tolerated if not welcomed; but even to him the leaves and the silence seemed to say: Keep out. Go back.

After a few moments, in which he kept quite still as if he were allowing the island time to recognize him, he moved over the rocks which led up steeply into the darkness above. The moonlight, filtering through the close leaves of a giant tamarind, showed the stones which were white with bird-droppings. These droppings, which had accumulated undisturbed through the years, were inches deep under his feet and gave out a strong smell of ammonia. He climbed slowly into an alien world. The trees round him were thick and close. From them came a subdued stirring and rustling. The faint moonbeams that penetrated the darkness showed only hanging leaves, but he knew that behind their screen the birds were ranked in serried rows along the branches. He was walking through a heronry, the largest of the three heronries on the island, a colony of night herons which long ago had taken possession of this grove of tamarinds. The whole island was a feathered sanctuary, a world of birds. This world, unsuspected by the mainland, was vulnerable, precarious, but so far untouched; the island was forgotten, buried by the jungle. Its steep, tree-covered, thorny slopes were seldom visited except by the Sadhu, Ram Kishen, and the small boy, Prem. Here the birds were in possession. Earth and rock, tree, and sky, even the river, were theirs.

The rock path ended at a level space overgrown by a tangle of bushes and creepers and backed by a low cliff and a dark wall of trees. In the centre of this moonlit clearing, rising from the scrub jungle, was a huge solitary rock, over twenty feet high, rounded at the top, which the rains had fluted, planed, and carved. Its bold and beautiful shape was edged with blackest shadow and displayed by the full light of the moon. The stone shone with bird-droppings, as did all the other boulders of the island; on its summit a large white owl was perched. The Sadhu paused and made a gesture of reverence towards this great stone, bird-possessed as it now was, and the owl spread its pale, moth-like wings and sailed as silently as a dream across the clearing into the darkness of the trees.

The Sadhu forced a way through the bushes and tangled

46

undergrowth, moving slowly and with difficulty. In the daytime this open glade was drowsy with sunshine and alive with
the flight and song of birds; butterflies hovered over the flowering shrubs and sunbirds flew from flower to flower. Even in the
sunshine the great, cold stone brooded over the place, and he
was always glad to leave it; but for the birds the glade was a
favourite nesting-place.

A narrow cleft, smelling of damp and birds' excreta, led up
the cliff face which was stained and discoloured by generations
of swallows that had built their clay nests there. In the darkness
these nests were invisible but when the Sadhu climbed from
the cleft on to the higher level, among trees and clumps of
bamboos, the moonlight, striped with shadow, fell on to an almost imperceptible path which only his feet had made. The
ground in front of him fell away to the further slopes of the
island and through the trees he could see the river and the chain
of islands, the tail of the snake, stretching away upstream; he
stood for a few moments gazing down at it; the rocks of the
nearest island and its one small clump of trees were clear in
the moonlight but the others were only dark shapes on the
pale water of the river. A silver and slumbrous peace lay over
the islands; all was quiet except for a nightjar's chuckling cry;
but the trees round him were thick and populous, with not only
two heronries and flocks of egrets but cranes and storks and
water birds, some rare and seldom found elsewhere. As he stood

47

there, the Sadhu knew that he had been observed and accepted as he always was, and then forgotten.

Dawn was not far off and the Sadhu had not yet done what he had come to do. He followed the rocks that led up on his right to the highest point of the island, from which he looked down a steep slope to the water below. Here the river was at its widest, a moonlit expanse across which even in the daytime the further bank was invisible. He crouched down on the rocks which were exposed and flattened and still held something of the day's warmth. Beneath him a single tree grew out of the rocks and leant over the river at a sharp angle. Its leafy crown was close below him. Among the leaves he could make out the dark shape of the eagles' eyrie, a large, shapeless mass of leaves and twigs formed into a rough nest. The eagles had reared their young in this safe and remote spot for many years. The parent birds knew him as he knew them. Year after year he had peered down at the pale eggs, watched the two naked fledglings, seen the first flight. Fishing eagles are not generally as shy and solitary as other eagles are but this pair was used to quiet and loneliness. Their wild hearts were fixed upon this place and tree but he knew that if they were often disturbed they would not hesitate to leave it. As he crouched above the tree, he could see the dark humped shape of the male bird perched apart from the home nest and a little above it. It must have known that he was there but it did not move. After waiting a few moments, he stretched out an arm towards it and gave a low, whistling cry.

The eagle still hesitated, half opening its great wings and folding them again, then, as the Sadhu repeated the familiar summons, it launched itself into the moonlight, circled once above the tree, planed down towards the rocks, and alighted a few yards away from the crouching man, landing silently, its curved, naked talons gripping the rock. In the moonlight, the light-grey head, whose long crown feathers were like untidy hair, with the bird of prey's fierce beak and glittering eyes, turned slowly towards the Sadhu, who sat motionless, his hand still extended, palm upwards, towards the bird.

Although the tales told in the villages of the Sadhu's power over snakes, birds, and all living creatures were generally believed, even those who knew him best would have been surprised by the moonlit scene that followed. Perhaps Ram Kishen and his child Prem would alone have accepted what they saw without feeling the cold touch of fear that comes with the inexplicable. These two had seen something of the Sadhu's way with living creatures and the child had a small part of the same power, which has been possessed by many men, saints among them, in greater or lesser degree. As for Ram Kishen, he was wild and fierce and shy as the eagles were, and had something of their intractability.

The bird slowly sidled closer to the outstretched hand. When it reached the Sadhu, it bent its head and waited, ruffling the feathers on its back, moving its wings slightly so that they seemed to shiver in anticipation. The hand descended gently, first on the grey head and then down to the darker back, soothing, caressing. That there was a power in the hand was clear. The tense, nervous alertness left the bird; the restless eyes remained hooded until the hand was slowly withdrawn. When the Sadhu began to speak, the eagle raised its head again, seeming to listen to the low sing-song words. Twice the great wings were spread and the bird rose into the air, the second time to descend not on to the rock but on to the man's outstretched arm, which the hard, scaly talons clasped lightly. The Sadhu held the bird's weight as if he did not feel it, slowly drawing his arm in towards his chest. In his nostrils was a strong fish smell. The warmth given out by the feathered body was on his skin. Bird and man confronted each other at close range, bird eye and human eye searching each other. Then the arm was stretched out again and the eagle left it, soaring high above the tree and plunging down again to perch on the rock where it had been.

The Sadhu looked down at the nest and called the low, summoning cry again. This he had to repeat twice before the female bird responded. The leaves of the tree were agitated in the moonlight and the branches shook. The odour of the nest, which held the fishbones and debris of many years, came up to him; it was stronger, less fish-like and clean, than the scent of the bird itself. A few feathers and twigs fell from the tree and then the female rose through the branches into the paleness of the sky and circled above him. Larger than the male and heavier, always more difficult and more shy, it took her some time to come down to the rock and perch close beside her mate. The Sadhu did not attempt to touch her then but addressed her in his soft voice, coaxing, pleading, until she moved sulkily and heavily over the rocks behind him and settled herself at his other side.

The Sadhu sat on the rock between the two birds, the three hunched shapes dark against the silver night, as he had often sat with them before, holding his arms round his knees, gently rocking himself backwards and forwards, sometimes crooning his soft song but for the most part silent, staring out over the river. If his companions could have understood his thoughts he might have said them aloud, stating his problem to the eagles, asking their opinion, for in it they and every living thing on the island were concerned.

He alone, a professed holy man, was against this religious project of the founding of an ashram and the building of a temple. The villagers and fishermen were delighted, seeing not only a source of employment and gain but a distinction to the neighbourhood. Even Hari, who he knew had already guessed his uneasiness and displeasure and had put it down to jealousy for his own temple and repute, was interested. Only Ram Kishen and Prem, who, being what they were, might not be allowed entry to the ashram temple—Krishna's temple from which no man however humble should be expelled—perhaps felt as he did, and he could not be sure of them. He, alone, was determined that the ashram should not be built and the peace of the islands disturbed. If the eagles had been capable of understanding, he might at that moment have told them his reasons. He might have said that in the long years of meditation and privation he had shed the rules and creed of any religion but he believed as the Hindus do that God is in all things, animate and inanimate, that all things are in God. To refrain from destruction as Hari did, and as the new ashram's founder, the good old man Mishra, hoped to do, was not enough, death being a part of life. What was needed was respect for every living thing, for its way of life and its right to its own place on the earth. Having reached this point in his thoughts, the Sadhu looked round at the dark, populous trees and then down at his two patient companions.

All over the world the birds were moving before the flood of men, pausing in this tree and that, this reed bed or forest, only to hear the sound of the axe and the approaching wheels and to move on, to go, as the green and the cover became less and less and more difficult to find and keep. At that moment the Sadhu made up his mind. Let the ashram, the monastery, the temple, the whole sacred dream rise on some other site. On these island rocks it was fitting that only the birds and a solitary like himself should perch.

The eagles, disturbed by the anger rising in him, moved uneasily at his side. He put his hands gently on their heads and by this contact soothed and quietened not only them but his own mind. When he stood up quietly, the eagles turned their heads to look at him. He bent down and touched each bird lightly once again, in farewell and dismissal. As they took off from the rocks, spreading their wings and rising together above the tree to watch him move away, he lifted his arms towards them and called a reassurance, a promise. This promise, made in the moonlight, he had no idea how to keep.

As the Sadhu glided swiftly back across the water, steering well out into the river until he was close to his own island, he kept an eye on Pratap Singh's distant lantern and watched for fishing-boats. He was later than he had meant to be. Dawn was competing with the moon when he tied his boat in its own bay again.

❋❋*❋* *Part Two*

Part Two

I

꙰꙰꙰ One morning two months later, at the end of December, a boat-load of five notables from the town disembarked on the new bamboo jetty beside the notice-board. They had come, by invitation, to see the progress that the new ashram had made. Hari Das Thirani was among them; the day was cold with a fresh, clear brightness and he wore his thickest brown coat, and a woollen scarf round his throat.

Hari knew that they had been asked to the island out of friendliness and enthusiasm, but he also knew that it was no coincidence that all five of the middle-aged or elderly gentlemen now standing on the jetty and looking round them were men of wealth and property. He knew very well that the building of even a small temple and ashram was an expensive undertaking at the best of times, that estimates were always exceeded and that unforeseen difficulties and needs appeared. Here the necessity of ferrying all materials and labour across the considerable stretch of water between the island and the shore almost doubled the cost. The local boatmen were prospering and Hari himself had made some profit out of the last consignment of cement, for instance. If he found himself sufficiently impressed with what he saw that day, the merchant had made up his mind to make a substantial donation to the new temple; even though it was a Hindu and not a Jain temple, merit would be acquired by such a gift, and he could well afford it. He looked, a little guiltily, at the Sadhu's island; across the water its rocks and trees were lit by the pale gold sun of winter. He was relieved to see that there was no sign of the holy man.

Dr. Mahabir Prasad Mishra was hurrying to meet them, his white hair, the skirts of his white muslin dhotie, and the fringes of his cream woollen shawl flying behind him as he advanced. He was a tall, thin old man, perhaps sixty-five years old, although the eager, glowing expression on his face and the speed of all his movements made him seem much younger. Hari had met him several times before, and although he had summed him up as an impractical dreamer and a rather silly old man, he could not help liking him. The man had the charm of complete un-

58

selfconsciousness, and round him was an aura of goodness and sincerity that could almost be felt. Behind him walked, more sedately, a short, small man with large, horn-rimmed spectacles and an expressionless face. In the breast pocket of his long-skirted coat, which was tightly buttoned up to the high collar, a fountain pen and two pencils were clipped and he carried a long roll of papers under his arm. This was Dr. Mishra's secretary, a Bengali, Bijoy Chandra Mukhopadhyaya.

The traditional greeting was given and the conducted tour of the island began. The flight of steps to the temple had been made up the great boulder and this they climbed, with the white-haired old man skipping up in front of them as lightly as a goat. Two sulky Brahmin priests with shaven heads and saffron-coloured cloths were already in residence, living very uncomfortably in the unfinished temple buildings. The main temple was almost complete. The image of the God, that of the Lord Krishna, the Blessed Lord, was installed on the raised dais or altar within the railed-off space, the inner room, the Sanctum Sanctorum, where no one might go. The lamps were hung and the scent of incense overlaid the damp, cold smell of new concrete. The party left their shoes on the narrow terrace at the top of the steps and crowded into the pillared outer room.

Those of them who had not visited the temple before were agog to see the by-now-famous footprint. There it was, to the right between two pillars, a short distance in from the edge of the floor. It was protected by a small square of iron fencing picked out in gold paint and was surrounded by offerings of flowers.

On the day of the footprint's discovery two months before it had seemed as if the Sadhu's plan, if plan his sudden impulse could be called, might succeed. When Dr. Mishra and his secretary had arrived by boat on the island they found it in an uproar; masons, workmen, coolies, boatmen were gathered round Pratap Singh, who had lost his temper and was brandishing his staff. At first in the confusion of voices the two gentlemen had made out nothing except that everyone on the island wished to leave it at once. But when they had seen the tools which had been discovered under the corrugated iron, the scattered cement, the other manifestations, and, finally, the footprint, uncovered to the sun and fixed for ever in the stone, they had not believed in such ignorant credulity even in such a rural backwater.

Trying to keep their tempers, they had explained that in these days no one believed in ghosts, bhūts or such-like, and that these existed only in the imagination. This had not had much effect, and when Dr. Mishra suggested that the print must have been made by one of the masons themselves, there were angry murmurs from the crowd, and the head mason, a thickset man, self-important and short-tempered, shouted that he was an honest man, that he had covered the concrete himself and had been the last to leave the place. When Dr. Mishra then said that someone—a mischievous boy perhaps, for the footprint was certainly small and slender—had visited the island in the night, Pratap Singh denied it vigorously. No one could have swum from the mainland or from island to island in such a strong current, and no boat had landed unseen. He had been awake and watchful all night and had patrolled the beach constantly. No one really believed Pratap Singh and a look of doubt had appeared on the faces of those gathered on the rocks round the new temple floor, until the head mason pointed out that the footprint was under the sacking and yet sharp and clear in every detail, which was indeed a mystery. How could a mere boy, who knew nothing of the plans of the temple, have known where to lay the offering of flowers? At once babel had broken out again and Dr. Mishra had wrung his hands in despair.

Suddenly a voice at the back of the crowd had mentioned the Sadhu. In the silence that then fell, everyone turned to look at the Sadhu's island.

Dr. Mishra had, of course, heard of the Sadhu and he asked eagerly if the man possessed a boat. A chorus of voices assured him that the holy man had not left the island for over thirty years. The single voice then reminded everyone of the Sadhu's ability to walk on the water when he felt inclined to do so. At this, before his secretary could stop him, Dr. Mishra had lost his temper. He stamped his foot and cried that if such credulous fools could believe that a man they all knew was part bird or part fish, they could believe anything and did not deserve such an ashram as his in their midst. Pratap Singh then declared loudly that, although everyone except strangers knew the Sadhu possessed unusual gifts, it had never been hinted that the holy man could make himself invisible, and that no one, no one at all, had landed on the island that night. When at last Pratap Singh's breath failed him, the head mason stepped forward. Pointing down at the footprint, he announced in a solemn voice that no mortal man had made it.

For the crowd, this had settled the question, and a move was made towards the boats. Dr. Mishra hurried forward as if to bar the way but, before he could speak, his secretary seized him by the tail of his muslin shirt and stepped in front of him. In a mild voice, but one that carried to the boats, he then announced that the head mason had spoken only the truth. The footprint had been made by a God.

Silence had fallen again, while Dr. Mishra stared at his secretary, who returned his look with a bland smile. Agitated murmurs then came from the crowd and a confused questioning which suddenly changed to shouts of joy. The crowd of workmen surged towards the site of the temple, eager to see again for themselves the miracle which had appeared among them. Pratap Singh, using his staff, forced them back and cleared a space for his employers. His black mustaches quivered scornfully, but he kept his opinions to himself and concentrated on showing off his strength and zeal. Several voices then demanded to know which of the Gods had made the print. Some shouted the name of the Lord Siva. Others called for Kali, Siva's consort, and an argument broke out as to whether the short and slender footprint could be that of a Goddess or not.

The secretary had raised his voice again, demanding silence and more seemly behaviour, and had insisted that everyone should listen to what he had to say. His voice, when he chose, was resonant and compelling and remarkably deep for such a small and puny man. He stood directly in front of Dr. Mishra, as if he wished to seem the mouthpiece of that impressive and even saintly but bewildered figure. When the secretary had the crowd's attention, he asked that everyone should seat himself and listen without interrupting. Like obedient children, the men checked their excitement and squatted down on the rocks. Only the head mason and Pratap Singh were left standing, and they folded their arms on their chests and prepared, each in his own way, to listen.

The secretary was a gifted speaker, as many Bengalis are. He had spoken simply, as was fitting for his audience, but eloquently. His words seemed to many who listened to him to be inspired, to fall from the blue sky above him as naturally and rightly as the sun's rays. Or if they did not think this at the time, they thought so later, when discussing and rediscussing the events of the day.

63

He had begun by pointing out to them that, as far as anyone knew, the Gods had taken no obvious interest in the island until the previous night, and that therefore it was the building of the new temple that had drawn their attention to the place. As they all knew, Dr. Mishra and his associates were Vaishnavas and the temple was to be dedicated to the worship of Krishna, the Blest of Beings, the Lord of the Senses, the best loved of the avatars of Vishnu, in his aspect as a young boy. Without any doubt it was the Lord Krishna himself who had paid a visit to the island in the night. It was natural that he should wish to see for himself the site of the new edifice which would rise in his honour. The Gods were seldom consulted before such a project was begun, and there must be many temples in the land that did not give much pleasure to those for whom they were built. How lucky, how blessed, everyone on the island was to know, by the grace of this footprint, made by one who could come and go without leaving a trace of his passage, that the site was certainly approved. The placing of the flowers on the altar was an added sweetness from one who was himself all sweetness and light. On the very spot where the flowers had lain, the image of the God, standing in the familiar posture with his flute to his lips and smiling his celestial smile, would soon rise for all to see. As for the other manifestations, it was well known that this God was a mischievous God, playful and fond of teasing, as the many stories concerning him showed. Was it not Krishna who had stolen

64

the butter and milk, raided the orchards of the herdsmen, hidden the bathing-women's clothes, and danced and played with the milkmaids in the pastures of Vrindavan? Was it not the Blessed Lord who in a gay mood had uprooted the mountain Govardhana and held it over the villages to save them from excessive rain? The footprint, the all-important footprint, could only have been made by Krishna. It must be guarded as the treasure it was. Dr. Mishra would order a suitably rich and decorative grill or fencing that would protect it from the too-pressing attentions of the devout. Meanwhile, he took it upon himself to suggest that a temporary protection of bamboo should be made at once.

At this point, Dr. Mishra, who had roused himself from his daze a few moments before and had been plucking at his secretary's sleeve, seized him by the shoulder and pulled him back. The old man looked both ruffled and annoyed; his white hair stood up like a crest. He waved his arm in a gesture of anger and repudiation but, before he could speak, the crowd's attention was diverted from him by the head mason, who stepped forward and in his turn made a short speech.

As the senior workman and one who acted as foreman, he was prepared to speak for all present when he said that they wholeheartedly accepted the Babu's neat explanation of the appearance of the footprint as it explained everything that had puzzled them and tidied away all loose ends. This was an occasion for prayer and rejoicing. Might he suggest that a day's holiday, with pay of course, be granted to everyone?

There were murmurs of approval from the crowd, which he silenced by lifting his hand.

One point, he said, had been overlooked. It was certain that the God approved of the temple's site, but surely they could not accept the moving of the sticks which had been placed to show where the other buildings would be merely as a mischievous prank? It was clear that Krishna did not approve of these sites and had chosen others. The choice in some cases seemed strange and would present many difficulties, but he was only a mason and could not argue with a God.

Dr. Mishra groaned as the secretary took his roll of carefully drawn plans from under his arm. They looked at each other in dismay, while a wave of rejoicing swept the island. Behind them, Pratap Singh leant on his staff, gazing vaguely about him while he strained his ears to hear what the two Babus, the gentlemen, were saying to each other.

The sound of happy voices and of laughter had reached to the other islands. It had come faintly to the Sadhu as he swept his courtyard and he had paused to listen thoughtfully. A cloud of birds had risen from their island and had hung uneasily above the trees as the laden boats set off one by one for the mainland, but for the rest of that day and the night that followed the islands had been undisturbed.

Now, two months later, standing in the completed temple, Hari stared down at the footprint. He had seen it before and he had his own ideas about it, but these he kept to himself. He raised his head and looked curiously at the faces of Dr. Mishra and his secretary. The old man was smiling his sweet and gentle smile. He radiated happiness and complacency as he told them of the difficulty they had experienced in working on the temple because of the hundreds of the devout who, in those first days, had flocked to the island. Perhaps he had really come to believe in some vague roundabout way of his own in the footprint's divine origin. The secretary's face gave nothing away. It was composed and grave, as it always was. He met Hari's eye, and even that astute man did not know what to make of him.

When at last they all emerged garlanded from the temple, Dr. Mishra conducted them up the steps and along the winding paths that had been made among the rocks, his long legs moving too fast for the elderly and portly men who panted after him. Everywhere workmen were busy, digging, moving stones, piling bricks, mixing cement, but although the island hummed with endeavour, there was not very much to be seen; foundations had been laid and a few walls begun. It seemed to Hari that these buildings-to-be were perched in unlikely and awkward places, either huddled close together or so far apart that they would have to be linked by long and costly flights of steps;

67

but, as he had heard the story of the God's interference in the matter of the sites, he understood why this was.

Behind and above the temple was a small, single-roomed cell-like building which was complete except for an upper storey that would be added later. Here Dr. Mishra already lived for days and nights at a time, although the cement of its walls and floors still oozed damp. Round it, between the rocks, a small garden had been made in which, besides the sacred Tulsi plant that grew close to the door, seedlings of marigold, salvia, and nasturtium were planted. A neat trellis of bamboo gave some privacy to the place and supported a convolvulous creeper whose morning-glory flowers of rich blue were wide under the sun. Dr. Mishra was obviously pleased and proud of this small and slightly ridiculous building. From its door he could look over the temple roof below him to the islands and the pearly gleam of the river. Here, he told the party, as they peered into the damp little room, in which there was nothing except a string cot, a roll of bedding, a black tin dispatch-box, and, in a niche in the wall, a small image of the Goddess Lakshmi, consort of Vishnu, he would find the peace and spiritual fulfilment which, in his old age, it was right that he should find.

Hari felt a pang of envy. Here was someone who was at the end of his search. Then, as he looked round at the unfinished buildings which crowded the little house and its minute patch of garden, he shook his head. Even when the workmen had gone and the ashram was complete and populated only by its novices and priests, it would be about as quiet and peaceful as an aviary or a beehive. As it was, the sound of a priest clearing his throat under the eaves of the temple below them could be plainly heard where they stood.

Although there was nothing more to be seen at present, Dr. Mishra was determined that they all should make the round of the island and be told his plans for the future. He led the way along a path which soon left the cleared part of the island and the workmen behind. The path along which the Sadhu had walked in the moonlight had been widened and the vegetation had been cut back, but it still wound up and down over the rocks and crossed huge boulders, and soon Dr. Mishra was asked to walk more slowly.

They passed several small dug patches of ground where corn would be sown, and the orchard of banana and guava trees. The fleshy arms of a clump of pagoda trees were bare and the bushes thin-leaved and touched by the brief Indian winter. Above their heads the hill went up against the blue sky. Someone asked what would be done with the Fakir's cave, but Dr. Mishra was busy explaining that he hoped to keep a few cows on the island, although he had been assured that when all the proposed buildings were finished there would not be enough vegetation left to satisfy one small calf and that the swim to the mainland and back every day would be too far. The old man talked without stopping as he walked. Every possible niche in the rocks was earmarked for some building, a classroom, a more extensive cookhouse, quarters for Brahmin cooks; it was only a matter of time, of levelling the ground a little, and of raising further funds.

The island was not large and before they realized it the party had completed the tour and were back on the slope above the latrines, looking down on the temple and jetty again. From here a path led straight up to the summit of the hill. It was Dr. Mishra's intention that they should all climb this hill to see the view over the river and the remarkable formation of the islands below whose rocks, he assured them, would appear from the height to be azure, cerulean, but after one glance at the path, this everyone declined to do. The old man was obviously disappointed, but Hari made them all laugh by suggesting that the future inmates of the ashram could keep in bodily as well as spiritual trim, in spite of the smallness of the island, if a rule were made that everyone must climb this path twice a day.

The secretary murmured that refreshments after their walk were waiting for them on the level ground by the jetty and, at a wave of Dr. Mishra's hand, he led the way down. As they descended the path in single file, they met a man carrying a bucket who stepped well to one side and waited until they had passed. Hari recognized Ram Kishen and acknowledged his exaggerated salaam with a nod of the head. Dr. Mishra noticed this exchange with surprise and explained that the man, who was very poor, was glad to earn a little by cleaning out the latrines every day. But when Hari, before he could stop himself, asked if the Untouchable, the Chandal, Ram Kishen, would be allowed to enter the temple, Dr. Mishra looked uncomfortable and answered that they could, of course, but changed the subject.

A carpet and improvised seats had been arranged in front of the watchman's hut above the beach. Here sweets and cool drinks were handed round. Hari, looking round him, saw that Pratap Singh, who usually spent the day on the mainland, was standing in the background but near enough to hear what was said. Several boats were moored to the jetty below them. In one, mending a net laid over his knees, sat the fisherman Govind. In another, of a more humble sort, was a small naked boy who was playing happily with a few sticks and a bunch of leaves. Hari, recognizing Govind and Prem, raised his eyebrows and looked across the water at the rocks of the nearer island. There was no need for the Sadhu to show himself. His allies and spies —among whom Hari, in spite of his interest in the ashram, supposed he should count himself—were assembled in force and each in his own way would put in a report.

The merchant smiled to himself and, standing up, prepared to take his leave with the rest of the party. As they waited to embark on the jetty, the secretary appeared at his elbow. In a persuasive and gentle voice he insinuated that any donation to

the temple would be welcome as expenses were far greater than
had been thought and although there were, of course, plenty
of funds still in hand these would not be enough to carry out all
Dr. Mishra's plans as they deserved.

Hari answered shortly—for he had suddenly decided that he
neither liked nor trusted this small man—that he would need
time to think this over. Dr. Mishra, hearing his name, turned
round and asked the merchant if he had enjoyed his visit and
what he thought of the ashram. His voice was gay and, looking
into the old man's happy face, it was impossible to believe anything but good of him.

Hari felt slightly confused between them both and he said
the first thing that came into his mind, which was that the
only criticism he had to make was that the island was too small
for such ambitious schemes.

For a moment Dr. Mishra looked disconcerted and then he
laughed and said that in that case they would have to ask permission of the Government to occupy yet another of the islands.
The Sadhu was already in possession of the nearest, and, of
the other five, four were too small and barren for their needs,
but the green island across the water belonged, he understood,
to no one. He and his secretary had already paid it a brief
visit. The place was steep and wild and overgrown. He must
confess that they had not gone beyond the beach. He had not
cared for the feeling or the atmosphere.

As he said this, his expression changed and became troubled and uneasy. His secretary made an impatient movement, quickly checked. Suddenly, from the boats tied immediately below them to the poles of the jetty, a child cried out shrilly.

Everyone turned and looked down. The small naked boy stood up in his boat, shaking his fist at them and yelling angrily. No one could make out what he said except that it was something to do with the bird island and that the word eagles was repeated again and again. Govind dropped his net and, leaning over the side of his boat, picked Prem up and held his hand over his mouth. Dr. Mishra asked what the trouble was, but the fisherman, keeping firm hold of the struggling child, shrugged his shoulders and did not answer. Hari laughed, and the visitors made their farewells a little too hastily. As their boat swung out on the current, they all turned to look at the bird island.

It lay green and quiet and withdrawn above its reflection in the water, seeming further away than it really was.

2

❦ The Sadhu was sitting in the pale afternoon sunshine in his customary place at the top of the steps. In the last months the island had seen few visitors. This he accepted philosophically, knowing that when the novelty of the ashram and the new temple had worn off the villagers would return. That afternoon he was to see only his regulars. Pratap Singh arrived first.

The tall, black-bearded Sikh followed the teaching of the Gurus and wore the long hair, the comb, the iron bracelet, the shorts, and the dagger, as all good orthodox Sikhs should do, but at heart he was a natural rebel and something of a renegade. He had known the holy man for many years and had come to love and reverence him as he did no other man. Although he never entered the temple, he liked to sit in the courtyard, which to him was the most peaceful place he knew and a contrast to his noisy, turbulent home and way of life.

Climbing the steps slowly and with dignity, his turban carefully wound, his shirt newly ironed, he went first to the courtyard, as he always did, perhaps to compose his mind before his talk with the Sadhu. In the boat on the beach below, he had left his staff and old army greatcoat and a basket of provisions for the night. He meant to go straight to the ashram island after his visit to the holy man, although he was not officially on duty until sunset.

The town had few attractions for Pratap Singh these days, and he went home only to eat and drink. Since his trouble over the driving-licence, he had lost face in the bazaar. He owed money, and his wife, who had always been a scold, nagged him ceaselessly, and his children were disrespectful. It was no wonder that he preferred the islands. At night, under the stars, they were quiet, empty of the shrill voices and importunities of women and the crying of children. Even when Dr. Mishra chose to stay after the boats had left, the Sikh could sleep most of the hours away in peace under the grass thatch of his hut. By day there was often something of interest going on, such as yesterday's visit of Hari Das Thirani and the other notables. On the island, as watchman, he was of some importance, trusted, consulted, and even liked, he believed, by his employer, who was a generous, pleasant, gullible old gentleman. Life would have been easy and profitable for Pratap Singh and everyone concerned with the ashram if only the secretary had not been there to watch every brick and nail, every plank of wood, every anna. Now the Sikh made an obeisance to the Sadhu as he passed him and entered the courtyard.

When, after some time, he reappeared, he was annoyed to see the fisherman Govind seated on the steps below the Sadhu and talking earnestly. Pratap Singh had wanted to be the first to tell the details of the visit of yesterday. He sat down and interrupted the old man at once. How could the fisherman, from his boat below the jetty, have seen and understood what was going on? He, Pratap Singh, had been standing close by and had heard every word and seen every gesture. He wondered if Mahabir Babu, as Dr. Mishra was generally called, knew that his secretary had gone from person to person asking in a shameless way for money for the ashram. In the beginning they had all been given to understand that there was money to burn.

Govind interrupted in his turn. From his lowly place in his boat he had heard the final conversation on the jetty which the Sikh could not possibly have heard. The two Babus had told the merchant in his hearing that they were going to build on the bird island, as the one they had was too small for their plans. How this was to be done he could not imagine. It would take months to clear the jungle, but if the Sadhu did not believe him, he could ask Hari Das Thirani himself.

The Sadhu looked at the two angry and jealous men thoughtfully. When he had first heard of the discovery of the footprint and of the scenes that followed, he had been more amused than annoyed and had taken the unfortunate results of his hastily improvised plan calmly, but the time had come to make another attempt to keep his promise to the eagles. He must go to work with what tools he had: his own brain and five human beings, three of whom, these two and Hari, he would have to use without their knowing it; they all had an interest or stake in the ashram and could not be expected to approve of his plans. He knew that Ram Kishen had not been allowed to enter the temple and that there had been an angry scene between him and the priests but, as far as the Sadhu knew, he was still working on the island. Perhaps only the holy man's fifth and smallest and weakest tool, the five-year-old Prem, would be wholly on the Sadhu's side.

Govind and Pratap Singh soon saw that the Sadhu was no longer listening to them. He sat beside them in his passive, listening attitude, with his hands relaxed on his knees and his eyes on their faces, but they knew that he had withdrawn into a region of his own. This did not disconcert them; it was to be expected of a holy man, and they assumed that he had been caught up and away from them by some spiritual wind. The truth was that the Sadhu's mind was concentrated on the practical aspects of his problem and was busy forming a plan; he made one, only to discard it, and then summoned up another. He did not notice when, after sitting silently beside him for some time, the two men rose together, made their farewell obeisances before him, walked quietly down the steps, entered their boats and rowed away in opposite directions.

The problem was a knotty one but, as the Sadhu wrestled with it, a vague but possible scheme began to form in his mind.

77

He brought his practised powers of concentration to bear on it, considering probabilities and details while the sun moved across the sky and the shadows of the leaves above him changed their patterns on the steps.

At last, he smiled and nodded his head, a little doubtfully, shrugged his shoulders and stretched himself. As his eyes focused again on his surroundings, he saw that Hari was sitting a few steps below him, waiting patiently with his plump chin on his hands and his silver-headed cane between his knees.

The merchant had come to the island to tell the Sadhu that he had decided to make a substantial donation to the new temple. There was no reason why he should not make this gift and no reason why the Sadhu should hear of it, but he knew that he would not feel comfortable and free of a faint sense of guilt until he had told him of his decision. When he had climbed the steps and seen that the holy man was deep in thought and unaware of his arrival, he had felt disappointed and taken aback, but he had waited for him patiently, sitting in the afternoon sunshine above the river.

Far away, across the broad main channel, the pelicans sunning themselves on a sandbank shone like grains of salt. A country-boat, high-sterned and low in the water under a load of golden straw, drifted past the island with the current, its great square sail slack and empty against the mast. A gariel, the harmless fish-eating crocodile, swam downstream at a furious rate with

78

only the shining round knob at the end of its long snout showing above the surface. Hari watched it idly until it was out of
sight and listened to the river lapping against the rocks below
him, while he waited for the peace that he found only in this
place to descend on him. Until the Sadhu stirred and spoke to
him, he forgot what he had come to say.

Almost unwillingly he roused himself, made his greeting, and
sat down again on the top step, but when the Sadhu heard his
news with calm indifference, as if the ashram were no longer
of any importance, Hari was surprised and annoyed.

He was still more surprised when the holy man suddenly
held out his cupped hands, as a beggar does and, in a beggar's
whine, asked if he and his humble island might also receive a
gift from such a rich and generous man, a few rupees instead
of hundreds would do for them. Hari looked at him suspi-
ciously. The Sadhu's eyes had a mischievous glint, but his face
was solemn and it was obvious that he meant what he said although he had never before asked the merchant for anything.
Hari took his purse from his pocket and dropped some coins
into the outstretched hands. When the Sadhu shook his head,
Hari added a note. The Sadhu's fingers closed over the money
and he turned to put it carefully under a stone by the wall.
Then, dismissing the ashram and its affairs with a wave of the
hand, he began to talk of other things.

Soon the two were involved in one of the discussions in

which the merchant delighted. He should have been altogether at ease and relaxed on this familiar ground but, sitting close to the Sadhu, he was dismayed to find that he was apart from him as he had never been before. At first he thought that the fault was his. He longed to know what possible need the Sadhu could have for his fifteen rupees, but even when he put all thought of the money firmly out of his mind, he did not feel the serenity and the warm peace and sense of well-being that the holy man usually gave to those near him, as a flower gives its scent. Hari, watching carefully, gradually realized that the Sadhu was not himself. The holy man's eyes were bright and wide open instead of half shut, as they usually were. His forehead, usually smooth and bland, was wrinkled, and he, who when seated was always so still, fidgeted, moving his hands. Even his voice was different, high and quick.

Shocked and puzzled, Hari searched for a reason for this change. It seemed to him that the holy man had lost something of his detachment and otherworldliness and was even physically coarser and heavier. He told himself that this was imagination, but he knew that if the Sadhu had been any other man, a business associate of his own, for instance, he would have said that the man was hiding a secret excitement, even considering a rather shady deal. Hari was not as annoyed as he might have been when he saw that their afternoon talk was to be interrupted. A boat had appeared round the rocks and was making for the beach where his own boat was drawn up on the sand.

When Ram Kishen saw the merchant at the top of the steps, he made his boat fast and sat down on the rocks and turned his back, but his son, who was perched eagerly in the bows, had no such inhibitions. Directly the prow touched the sand, Prem scrambled ashore and ran up the steps to the Sadhu. The child was wearing a pink cotton shirt, bought in the bazaar with the earnings from the ashram, the first sewn garment that he had ever possessed. Prem had been waiting for several hours to show it to the Sadhu but, when he reached the holy man who held out his arms to him, he forgot it, as he had already forgotten the bamboo cage under a cloth in the stern of the boat, although he had put it carefully there himself. He sat on the Sadhu's lap, leaning contentedly against the holy man's shoulder, and stared at the merchant with his sharp, small, black eyes.

Hari, who had many grandchildren and was mildly fond of all children who were under five years old and attractive as well as small, smiled at him, but Prem did not smile back. He had recognized the merchant as one of the party who had stood on the jetty the day before and now he scowled and, putting up his hand to draw the Sadhu's face down to him, whispered in the holy man's ear, pointing at the merchant and watching him as if he were dangerous. The Sadhu smiled and whispered back reassuringly, but Hari, annoyed by these intimate exchanges as much as by the child's obvious dislike of him, began to talk more loudly than he usually did of Dr. Mishra's plans for the bird island.

The merchant knew nothing of the reasons for the Sadhu's interest in this island but he had sensed long ago that it was of importance to him. If he now hoped to provoke the holy man into showing his feelings, he was disappointed. The Sadhu, still smiling, said politely that it was kind of Hari to give him this information but he had already heard it from both Pratap Singh and Govind. Prem interrupted him. Scrambling down from the holy man's lap, he stood in front of Hari, shaking a small, clenched fist, and yelling at him, much as he had done the day before from the boat. The Sadhu pulled him back by the pink shirt and held him firmly. When Prem's rage subsided and he stopped kicking and struggling, the Sadhu told him gently to go and fetch the cage from the stern of the boat and to bring the wounded bird to him.

The wounded bird? Hari turned to the Sadhu, raising his eyebrows and spreading his hands out in an exaggerated gesture of bewilderment, but Prem, after looking for a moment into the holy man's face, more in awe than astonishment, ran off down the steps, calling out to his father.

The Sadhu laughed and, stretching himself, crossed one leg over his knee, swinging his foot as he often did. The child, he explained, was fond of playing on the bird island, where his father, while he worked at the ashram, would often leave him out of harm's way to watch the birds as he liked to do. It was surely understandable that Prem should not want his playground and playmates disturbed. As for the cage, this was no display of miraculous powers, as Hari seemed to think. He had seen it in the stern as the boat approached the beach and, as it was covered by a cloth, he had known that it must hold an ill or a wounded bird. Hari smiled in his turn, shrugged his shoulders and, staring at the small, swinging foot close to him, said rather disagreeably that, miraculous powers or not, he was beginning to understand several things that had not been clear before.

For a few moments they looked at each other, Hari still smiling, the Sadhu expressionless. Then the Sadhu leant forward, gently patted the merchant's knee and, putting his head back, laughed his gay, sweet, ringing laugh again. The child came hurrying back up the steps with Ram Kishen behind him carrying the cage, and for that afternoon at least there was nothing more to be said.

The cage was carried into the courtyard and set down on the ground. Ram Kishen, at a wave from the Sadhu's hand, withdrew a little and seated himself on the balustrade above the river. Hari, forgotten, lingered by the temple and watched as the child and the holy man squatted down with the cage between them and removed the cloth which covered it. It was Prem who, at a word from the Sadhu, put his hand into the cage and drew out the unresisting bird, a plump brown mynah, and set it down on the beaten-earth floor.

The bird made no attempt to escape but stood on its unbroken leg, turning its head to look with bright, impertinent eyes from the man to the child. When the Sadhu picked it up to examine its injury more closely, it lay back in his hand, opening and shutting its yellow beak but showing no sign of fear. Prem did not try to be quiet or to keep still. He ran to fetch the Sadhu's broom and broke off a twig and handed it to the holy man, keeping up a loud prattle, describing to him and to his father how he had found the bird under the bushes close to the jetty of the ashram, and insisting that its leg had been broken by a stone thrown by some wicked and unnatural man, although the Sadhu reminded him that Mahabir Babu allowed no living thing to be killed or hurt on his island.

The Sadhu pulled several strong, shining, black hairs from his head and, with Prem's help, set the bird's leg. To Hari, it was clear that they had done this between them before. When all was finished, the hairs strongly knotted to bird leg and broom twig, the bird was put back in the cage and Ram Kishen sent to fetch water and grain from the back rooms of the temple. The Sadhu stood up to hang the cage between two plants under the shelter while the child danced round him, declaring in his shrill treble that directly the leg was healed he would take the bird across the water and let it go on the island of the birds, where, of course, it would live safely ever after.

Hari, unnoticed, went away, leaving the Sadhu sitting with Ram Kishen and Prem in the middle of the courtyard, while behind and above them the bird hopped about its cage, as it picked up the crushed grain. It seemed to him, as he turned his head for a last look at the courtyard, which was filled with gold light from the setting sun, that, now that he had removed himself from the scene, the three had drawn close together, as if they were plotting some secret move.

3

𝄞 Nine days passed before the Sadhu made his next attempt on the ashram. The time was needed for preparation. His plan was elaborate and difficult to carry out and, although he refused to admit it, risky for all concerned. He also refused to admit that it might not succeed, and he hid his doubts not only from his two willing accomplices but from himself.

Hari had been right when he sensed that the Sadhu was not himself. The holy man's mind was clouded by anger and obstinacy. That afternoon in the courtyard, after the merchant had left, Ram Kishen had told him that the eagles were not nesting that year as they usually did. The grey-headed fishing eagle will lay its two white, oval eggs in the same nest in the same tree year after year, between November and the beginning of March but most usually in December; never before had this pair left it so late; now, in January, they were still circling uneasily over their tree, occasionally adding to the huge platform of sticks which was their nest, but failing to settle. This last news came immediately after Ram Kishen's account of his expulsion from the temple which, until then, he had not been able to bring himself to tell even to the Sadhu.

If Ram Kishen had approached the temple and the priests in a suitably humble and patient way, perhaps he might have

86

been allowed on to the terrace and even into the outer room for a sight of the Gods, but he had marched up the steps as if he had a right to be there. He was a strong man, but the habits of obedience and awe were stronger; Dr. Mishra, who might have taken his part, was in the town and, with only a show of resistance, Ram Kishen had allowed himself to be driven out and hustled ignominiously down the steps by the priests and the secretary, with the assistance of the head mason. Although he had shouted from his boat that he would go to the police, complain to the magistrates, everyone who had heard him knew that he would do nothing.

When the Sadhu had listened to all that Ram Kishen had to say, he decided to put his plan into action at once. The next day Ram Kishen made an expedition to the mainland, not to the small town, where his doings might be noted and remembered but, getting a lift in a lorry full of half-cured hides, to a larger town twenty miles away by road. He took with him Hari's fifteen rupees securely tied in a rag.

The Sadhu, even to further his plan, could not bring himself to use the donations given him coin by coin through the years which, except for the small amount he used for his needs, had accumulated in the cloth bag which hung from its nail in the inner room; this was sacred money, set apart. It had been a happy inspiration to ask the merchant for alms that day. Each of his five tools, including the unknowing ones, must play a part in the preservation of the islands. It was lucky that Ram Kishen's expulsion from the temple had come, if it had to come, when it did; there was now no longer any doubt of his willingness to help the Sadhu in his schemes. The Sadhu only hoped that the money would be enough for the journey and the necessary purchases. Fifteen rupees seemed a fortune to him, but he had been out of the world for so long that money had no meaning.

Ram Kishen came back three days later, his old black boat making the crossing in the early dawn before even Govind was abroad. He brought with him Prem, a knife, a spade, several round, flat, covered baskets of unusual size and shape, some large earthenware pitchers, pieces of cloth, and some strange but necessary information. He and the child and the Sadhu, having hidden the Harijan's boat among the rocks, passed through the temple and were not seen again for several days.

During this time Hari visited the island three times. He was curious and uneasy. Twice he found the steps and the court-yard empty except for the mynah in its cage. The third time, when he arrived, Govind was waiting on the beach and Pratap Singh was coming down the steps. The Sikh had seen no sign of the Sadhu although he, too, had been several times to visit him. While he was in the courtyard, he thought that he had heared distant music, a flute or a pipe, but could not make out where the sound came from. The fisherman, when questioned, answered rather surlily that he had seen the Sadhu a few days ago and that the holy man had been as he always was, although he had asked for an extra supply of milk to be brought to the island and had given money and a new earthenware pitcher for this purpose. Hari, shaking his head, went away and left the island to its own devices.

The river ran as placidly as it always did at that time of year past the islands under the blue, cold-weather skies. The sun shone gold and clear from sunrise to sunset. The fishermen cast their nets, the porpoises played, the skeins of geese and arrow-shaped flights of duck wheeled across the skies. Water birds, egret, plover, tern, storks, and cranes waded in the shallows. The crocodiles lay basking on the sandbanks, and turtles scooped their shallow nests and laid their round eggs in the hot sand. The country-boats drifted past with the current and the squat beetle shapes of the river steamers left their wakes on the smooth water. The life of the river went on as it had always done. Only the islands were disturbed by unusual activity.

On the island of the ashram, as it was now called, the old Fakir being temporarily forgotten, the new buildings went up with remarkable speed. Many, if flimsy and without adequate foundations or any foundations at all, were finished. Dr. Mishra's house had acquired a second storey of one room and a latticed veranda. The island's vegetation had been cut back and uprooted until, except for the orchard and a few patches of cultivated ground and Dr. Mishra's garden, there was scarcely a bush or tree to be seen and no cover for anything larger than a mouse. Many new workmen had been enrolled and the place was noisy and as populated as a hive all day, although at night only Pratap Singh, Dr. Mishra, and the two Brahmin priests slept there.

Dr. Mishra and his secretary, encouraged perhaps by donations received from Hari Das Thirani and others, had paid another visit to the bird island. They had climbed the rocks, accompanied by a hoarse chattering that came from the unseen birds in the tamarind trees. They had advanced as far as the glade before the great stone. The sun had shone on them through the leaves and from the bushes had risen a sweet scent to drown the acrid smell of bird-droppings, but they had found it inconvenient to linger there and, speaking in whispers and looking over their shoulders, they had hurried back to their boat.

The eagles circled continuously above their island, rising and falling in wide watchful sweeps. The other birds, too, were disturbed. The whole island, under its green, was uneasy with twitterings and rustlings, and a cloud of birds, rising up from the trees and sinking back again, would frequently appear. The Sadhu's island gave no sign that anything unusual was going on. From the river it looked exactly as it had always done, although Ram Kishen's empty boat was often to be seen on the beach below the steps. But, in the centre of the island, hidden from the river by the trees, the Sadhu and Ram Kishen and Prem with them were very busy indeed.

It was a considerable undertaking to dig out, entice, and catch the snake population of the island and, having caught the greater part, to feed and keep quiescent, if not content, the coiled inmates of the baskets, bags, and pitchers, and of the bamboo cages that Ram Kishen had made and that were placed on the ledges among the rocks until the time came to put the second part of the plan in motion. Six days were spent in these preparations and then the real work began.

The Sadhu might more easily have captured some of the snakes at night in the rock chamber by the light of his fire when they came for their evening milk, but, thinking of the many quiet and happy nights that he and they had spent together, he felt that this would be too great a betrayal of their trust. He preferred to let Ram Kishen dig them out in their hidden lairs, or to squat himself on the warm sand in the sunshine with the snake-charmer's pipe to his lips until, drawn from their holes and hiding-places by the thin, sweet music or, as some think, by the vibrations released on the air, as well as by the promise of milk, they came to him one by one. Behind him, Prem, with the empty bags, and Ram Kishen, holding a stick, waited to do their part.

It was Ram Kishen's task to pin the reptiles to the ground

with a stick held close behind their heads until the Sadhu picked them up and examined them. The Sadhu allowed no one but himself to handle the harmful snakes, which he did without fear. Ram Kishen believed that the holy man was immune to their poison; for himself and Prem he had great faith in the snake-stone which he kept at hand in case of accidents. He went about his task silently and stoically, but he did not like it. In spite, or because, of all he had learned from the band of snake-charmers whom he had journeyed to find and from whom he had bought the round baskets, the snake-stone, and other implements of their trade, he was uneasy at the work. He did not think, as the Sadhu apparently did, that no snake would attack anyone or even bite unless deliberately provoked. He was angry because the holy man refused to allow him to break the fangs of the poisonous snakes, as the snake-charmers had taught him to do. The Sadhu would only agree to extract the poison at the last possible moment before embarking on the second part of his plan by forcing the snakes to strike again and again at a bunch of leaves until their venom had gone. Ram Kishen considered this precaution more or less useless and he was full of foreboding.

They had decided to starve the snakes who, in any case, ate only at long intervals, for as many days as possible, and then to feed them to repletion. The Sadhu hated to know that his snakes, resentful and surprised at the strange treatment they were receiving, were also growing hungrier every day. As the work went on, and the number of captives grew, he became more and more gloomy. It was only his new obstinacy that prevented him from abandoning his scheme, which he began to see was not only dubious but risky and perhaps foolish.

Of the three conspirators, Prem alone enjoyed himself during those nine days. He refilled the saucers of milk which were set in front of likely holes, and he was adept at catching frogs and putting them into pitchers in readiness for the snakes' meal. Prem possessed a part of the Sadhu's gifts and had no more fear of snakes than he had of any other living thing. He thought them beautiful and entertaining and he liked to feel their cool, dry, slightly rough bodies in his hands, but his affection was concentrated on birds and he felt no compunction over the snakes' capture, any more than he felt remorse at the necessary sacrifice of the frogs he caught for them. He was happy to be on the island for days on end with his father and the Sadhu and he left it reluctantly at night for the boat which, at sunset, would be anchored by a rope tied to a large stone off the beach in the slack water below the island. Here Ram Kishen and Prem would eat their evening meal and sleep under the stars.

The Sadhu passed his nights uneasily, rising from his crouching position by the fire in his rock chamber, where now only the great rat snake still kept him company, to make sure that none of his temporary prisoners had escaped and that all was well with them. The nights passed slowly for him who always before had found their dark peace too short, and he was glad when the dawn brought the child back to the island; Prem's enjoyment made what they were planning to do seem more reasonable.

When the ninth evening came, all was ready. Coiled in the baskets and the cotton bags and the cool depths of the earthenware pitchers was a surprisingly large number of snakes, although the poisonous among them were few; besides the cobras, all that the island yielded was a viper, five small, dark kraits, and a pair of banded kraits, whose yellow-and-black barred lengths could be trusted to be conspicuous and terrifying. Besides these formidable ones were rat snakes, a host of harmless grass and wolf snakes, whose combined presence would, the Sadhu hoped, be sufficiently intimidating. The poisonous snakes had spent their venom, and every snake was heavy with food and milk; to the milk a pinch of powder supplied by the snake-charmers had been added which, it was hoped, would keep the creatures drowsy and disinclined to move for some time.

For the first time in their lives, Ram Kishen and Prem stayed on the island after sunset. They waited on the beach while the Sadhu on his rock perch chanted his evening hymn. As darkness fell, he retreated to the temple and left them for a while alone.

Ram Kishen lit a small fire by his boat and cooked their rice which, with a few vegetables added, made their evening meal. Time must pass before, in the dead hours of the night, they would be summoned, but Prem at first could not sleep. Shivering with cold and excitement, he sat upright by the boat, as if the call might come at any moment, until his father scooped a hollow for him in the beach, persuaded him to lie down in it, and heaped the sun-warmed sand over his body. The night was cold and Ram Kishen kept the fire going and, long after the child was asleep, sat beside it with his arms round his knees, staring out at the dark river and the reflection of the stars.

The Sadhu's low whistle sounded from the steps soon after midnight. Ram Kishen woke Prem and brushed the grains of sand from the child's naked body. Without a word they climbed the steps and disappeared.

There was no moon and now, to add to the obscurity of the night, a mist began to rise from the river, shrouding the long chain of islands and veiling the stars. In the darkness there was a coming and going through the still darker room of the temple to the beach. When at last the laden boat, with the Sadhu in the prow in front of the carefully arranged pile of bags and baskets and Ram Kishen and Prem in the stern, put out from the beach, it moved like a shadow round the side of the island away from the main current and crept slowly along the fringe of rocks. The paddle handles had been muffled with rags and the boat itself had been well soaked with water so that its wood should not creak. Under the lee of the island it was invisible and when, after what seemed a long time, it crossed the open stretch of water between the two islands, mist lay between it and the light of the stars, and it could not have been seen even if there had been anyone awake to see it. This was the dangerous part of the journey, for here they must paddle hard against the current to reach the beach beyond the jetty. The disturbed water swirled and splashed at every stroke until it seemed that Pratap Singh, asleep in his hut, must hear them and come rushing out, lantern in hand.

The lantern remained where it was on the ground before the hut. Its small circle of light did not touch the jetty or the beach and the rest of the island was lost in darkness. The boat touched the sand with scarcely a sound.

Pratap Singh's snores rose and fell on the night and were echoed faintly from Dr. Mishra's house where the old man lay asleep in his new top room with his shawl wrapped round his head, and from the cell-like rooms behind the temple where the two Brahmin priests were rolled like cocoons in their blankets. No one saw or heard anything unusual. There was nothing to be seen except vague shadows moving in the mist and the darkness, flitting from the boat to the temple and in and out of the buildings, and there was little to hear: a few faint clinks and rustlings, the touch of bare feet on stone, a soft plop or two, and the creak of a basket lid. The shadows came and went for some time, but when the boat pushed off from the beach as silently as it had come, there was still no sign of dawn in the dark sky.

The conspirators returned even more silently than they had come, dropping swiftly back on the current. There was nothing more to be done except to wait and see what the next morning would show.

In the first light, the mist still lay coiled round the seven islands, waiting for the sun to disperse it, but Dr. Mishra woke at his usual time. Every day at five o'clock he would begin his morning ritual and bathe from the new steps of the temple, immersing himself and chanting the text to the sun. He folded his shawl and rolled up his bedding and, wearing only a dhotie and his sacred thread, he prepared to climb down the ladder, which led from his veranda to the garden below, when he was startled by a loud cry from the temple and the sight of one of the priests bounding through the mist down the steps to the beach.

Dr. Mishra hurried down the ladder and across his strip of garden, nearly stepping on a small snake which lay across the path. As he avoided it and opened his bamboo gate, another snake, larger, and bright green in colour, wriggled into a clump of salvia and disappeared and, as in a few steps he reached the lower terrace, yet another snake, coiled at the foot of a rock, lifted its head to hiss at him as he passed. At the entrance to the temple, he collided with the second priest, who stood transfixed, staring at the altar. Dr. Mishra looked over his shoulder and cried out in his turn.

Seen at close range and unexpectedly, a cobra is a shock. The Sadhu and Ram Kishen had chosen the temple as the centre of their stage and here they had deposited one of their chief performers, the female cobra, but they could not have foreseen that the male of this pair, which they had left in another building some distance away, would bestir itself enough to join its mate in the night. Now one great snake lay stretched along the altar ledge below the smiling image of the God while the other, in the centre of the stone floor, lifted a length of body from its coils, extended its spectacled hood, and swayed to and fro in an alarming manner. Dr. Mishra and the priest left the temple to its present occupants and fled down the steps to the jetty, where they found the first Brahmin and Pratap Singh talking agitatedly together.

Pratap Singh, woken by the priest's cry, had seized his staff and rushed out of his hut. It had taken him a few moments to understand what the commotion was about and then, long stick in hand, he had started towards the temple. As he passed his hut, he had remembered that he was barefoot which, in the island's present state, had not seemed wise. Bending down, he had reached for his shoes, which always stood together near his pillow, and had started back hurriedly; among his disturbed blankets, a rat snake was comfortably coiled.

He had sworn loudly and, backing out of the hut, had lifted his stick, only to find his arm caught and held by the priest. The two had then retreated to the jetty, where the Brahmin reminded the Sikh that the Nagas, the snakes, were sacred and worshipped by Hindus and that in any case he must not kill on the island.

Dr. Mishra, standing on the jetty, upheld this rule firmly even when, some hours later, the priests began to weaken and to suggest that perhaps, if they all looked the other way, Pratap Singh might be allowed to do what he thought best. All four had made several sorties on to the island, penetrating as far as the temple and to Dr. Mishra's house, in an effort to find some clothes and food. Each time they had retreated hurriedly. It seemed that the snakes were in possession.

The reptiles, still heavy with the plentiful meal of the evening before and still drowsy with the drugged milk, were sluggish and disinclined to move from the vantage points where the Sadhu and the others had placed them. They lay across the thresholds of the complete and half-finished buildings and on the piles of bricks and across the paths, and occupied the temple. As the sun rose, the four human beings on the jetty watched them moving languidly across the rocks into the warmth of the sunlight. It seemed to them that the island was alive with snakes.

When the first boatloads of workmen arrived from the mainland, they were hailed from the jetty and a confused argument began in which further boatloads joined as they arrived on the scene. The secretary, rowed by Dr. Mishra's two boatmen from the town, reached the island soon after nine o'clock, but no one had landed. He at once took charge and directed that small parties should land at different points round the island and, proceeding with caution and remembering that on no account must violence be used, should discover the extent of this invasion, if invasion it was and not, as he himself thought, a sudden appearance for some unknown reason of those who had been on the island all the time. This plan might have succeeded, for the snakes were not as many as they appeared to be, except that possible landing-points were few among the huge boulders and that every beach and slope had been carefully prepared by the Sadhu and his assistants. Each party in turn retreated hurriedly to its boat and those few bolder spirits, led by Pratap Singh, who had made a frontal attack and climbed the path behind Dr. Mishra's house as far as the latrines and the slope to the hill, also returned faster than they had set out to report that the snakes were everywhere.

The boats collected together again in a close bunch round the jetty, and the secretary disembarked with the head mason. Facing them, the two priests stood passively behind Dr. Mishra. The old man, his white hair shining in the sunshine and wearing his cream-coloured shawl, which Pratap Singh had bravely retrieved for him from the upper room, stood firm in the clamorous crowd which surrounded him. He repeatedly shook his head, and then he raised his arms to demand silence and made a short speech.

Dr. Mishra reminded the crowd of the great serpent Ananta, sometimes called Shesha, the thousand-hooded one, the chief of the serpents, on whose coils the Lord Vishnu slumbers above the sea of milk. Was it not this same Shesha who had gone before Krishna's earthly father when he carried the new-born babe away from the anger of the demon to the herdsman who was to be the Blessed Lord's foster father? And was it not Vasuki, the serpent, who was reborn as Balaram, the brother of Krishna?

When Dr. Mishra paused for breath, the secretary declared in his resonant voice that serpents were also evil. Was not the cobra Kaliya, who represents sin, subdued after a long struggle by the boy Krishna himself? The two gentlemen were listened to in respectful silence, although the clamour soon broke out round them again. The sound of the furious discussion that then took place reached to the nearer islands.

The Sadhu listened anxiously. Before dawn he had hidden himself among the rocks on the shore of his island where, as the mist thinned, he could see what was happening across the water. He watched the priests make their hurried exits from the temple and Dr. Mishra climb down his ladder with interest and satisfaction, but when Pratap Singh emerged from his hut, waving his staff, and the first argument took place on the jetty he began to feel uneasy. After the secretary arrived on the scene and the landing operations took place, he became really alarmed. He was forced then to admit to himself that only Dr. Mishra's beliefs and scruples stood between the lives of his snake parishioners and the workmen's sticks and stones. The Sadhu could, of course, hear nothing of what was being said on the jetty but, watching carefully, he tried to guess how the last argument was going.

At this point Ram Kishen in his boat, with Prem in the bows, appeared casually round the corner of the island and drifted close in behind the boats already crowded together at the jetty. Govind, having arrived soon after the workingmen, was already seated in his boat, listening unashamedly while he busied himself with his nets. The Sadhu knew that later in the day he would hear at least two versions of what had taken place and detailed reports of all that had been said, but he could not bring himself to go away. He stayed where he was, crouched between two rocks, as the sun climbed up the sky.

Soon after midday, the secretary, losing his temper, summoned his boatmen and was rowed quickly away towards the town. The boats drew away from the jetty and departed for the mainland while Ram Kishen let his boat drift discreetly away. Pratap Singh and the two priests were left with Dr. Mishra on the jetty, but not for long. After further argument, during which the Sadhu saw the old man stamp his foot and shake his head angrily, the others embarked in Govind's boat. For some time longer they lingered near the jetty, paddling a short way out and returning again for further attempts to make Dr. Mishra leave the island, but at last they, too, rowed off towards the town and the old man was left alone.

This the Sadhu had not foreseen, and now he became seriously worried. He had gambled on his certainty that Dr. Mishra would refuse to allow the snakes to be touched and he had guessed that, as no work could be done while the snakes were in possession, the island would be abandoned, but it had never occurred to him that Dr. Mishra would refuse to leave with the others. It was past midday already and night would come. Too late, he saw that he had taken a terrible risk.

The Sadhu left his hiding-place between the rocks and stood openly on the shore, but Dr. Mishra did not glance in his direction. After standing for some time on the jetty with his head bent, as if in prayer, the old man wrapped his shawl carefully about his shoulders and walked slowly but resolutely up the steps and disappeared into the temple.

Ram Kishen and his boat had vanished. The Sadhu went back across the rocks and along the winding paths and through his own temple, but the beach below the courtyard was empty. He tried to occupy himself with his daily tasks, but he soon found himself standing on the rock ledges again and looking across the water at the other island.

During the afternoon, Hari Das Thirani's boat came in sight and the Sadhu hid again. On board was not only the merchant himself and his boatmen but Pratap Singh. The boat came alongside the jetty but no one disembarked. After repeated shouts from the boatmen, Dr. Mishra showed himself on the terrace and, as Hari stood up in the boat and waved to him, came slowly down the steps. To the Sadhu, it was clear that the old man was determined not to leave the island, in spite of the merchant's entreaties. Pratap Singh, holding his coat and staff, climbed on to the jetty, but Dr. Mishra waved him back. Hari threw his hands up in despair and the boat cast off. The Sadhu hurried back through the temple and barely had time to don his square of red silk and to seat himself in his afternoon pose on the steps before Hari and his boat reached the beach.

The Sadhu that afternoon spoke little. He sat, composed and still and expressionless, listened, and gave no sign of his inward agitation. He heard the story of the plague of snakes with polite attention and shook his head and sighed when told of Dr. Mishra's intention to keep vigil that night alone in the temple, where, the old man had insisted, Krishna would protect him, and of his refusal to allow Pratap Singh or anyone else to stay with him on the island (not that anyone except the Sikh had offered to do so). Pratap Singh was hurt when the Sadhu did not comment on his bravery, and Hari was annoyed at his apparent indifference to these remarkable events. Later, Govind joined the party and, leaving his boat on the beach, climbed the steps, squatted down, and repeated the whole story again. The three discussed the situation and Dr. Mishra's chance of surviving the night while the Sadhu sat silent and immobile beside them, with his eyes on the river.

He was wondering where Ram Kishen had gone. His mind felt heavy and dull. He had lost his power of seeing with an inner eye what he needed to see, but he knew that Ram Kishen, whose resentment against the ashram smouldered and grew every day, was keeping out of sight on purpose, having guessed that the holy man might change his mind and wish to undo what had been done, perhaps even to retrieve the snakes, if that were possible. While the others talked and Hari took out his silver box of betel leaves, lime, spices, and areca nuts, and passed it round a little condescendingly, the Sadhu considered if this could still be done; but it was already evening, and what must be must be.

When his visitors had gone, the Sadhu followed his evening ritual, chanted his hymns as the sunset deepened round him and prepared for the night; but his heart was heavy with fear and anxiety and that evening he knew no exultation or release.

The night was clear and cold. He lit a fire in the rock chamber earlier than he usually did and sat close over it. His ancient rat snake kept him company but he could not sleep; his thoughts were on the ashram island where, across the water, Dr. Mishra was passing the night wrapped in his shawl and sitting in the middle of the temple floor in the circle of light cast by Pratap Singh's lantern. The night was long and, as the slow hours passed, the old man nodded and slept, but the Sadhu could not sleep. He sat by his fire staring into the flames.

If he had only known it, there was no need for his fears. During the course of the night, in search perhaps of their own earth and of the milk and the warmth of the fire they were used to, most of the snakes braved the cold river and of their own free will returned.

4

The third and last assault against the ashram on behalf of the eagles was launched only a few weeks later. The Sadhu had accepted the fiasco of the snakes calmly. For a day or two he was busy trying to make some sort of roll-call among them. This was difficult, as the snakes did not all return on the same night; a few lingered for a while among the rocks, and he was never to be certain that the muster was complete and that some had not decided to stay on the ashram island, keeping tactfully out of sight, or that a few had not been carried downstream by the current to land elsewhere. But by the third night he was sure that all those snakes known to him personally, which included the cobras and kraits and the other dangerous ones, were with him again. That night the circle round his fire was, as far as he could tell, complete. The snakes appeared to bear no malice for the handling they had received or for their uncomfortable adventure. They accepted the milk and the music he gave them and gathered close round him, as they had always done.

His relief at knowing that Dr. Mishra was safe and that no one, human or reptile, was any the worse, was greater than his disappointment at his failure or his annoyance at the results of his unfortunate plan. The prestige of both Dr. Mishra and the ashram was greatly increased. The old man only claimed that he had kept his vigil and prayed all night and that the God had heard his prayers and had caused the snakes to vanish as mysteriously as they had come, but his followers, headed by his secretary, were not content with such a simple explanation.

Soon highly coloured accounts of the snake invasion of the island, of Dr. Mishra's courage, and of the God's actions, were spreading through the countryside. Boat-loads of the curious and the devout again rowed out to the island. Everyone was eager to see the spot where the saintly old man had wrestled all night with cobras until the God, materializing suddenly, larger than life and bright blue in colour and surrounded some said by flames and others by an unbelievably sweet scent of flowers, had caused the reptiles to vanish at the first notes of his flute. A few sceptical voices were raised and Dr. Mishra himself at first tried to deny these stories. He was muddled and doubtful in his mind as to what exactly had happened, but it seemed to him that he had sat afraid and cold all night below the altar, with his eyes shut for fear of what they might see, and that nothing had touched him or come near him and that, before dawn, he had slept and wakened to find that he was indeed alone. No one took any notice of what he said. It was clear that this island, of all the seven, was an especially holy and potent place. The pilgrimages increased; money and offerings flowed in and were received by the secretary; the zeal and speed of the workmen grew every day, and a party of ten young novices arrived and occupied one of the finished buildings. The island, which for a day and night had been strangely peaceful and silent, hummed again like a busy hive.

Ram Kishen's reactions to the failure of their conspiracy were very different from those of the Sadhu. He had taken the snakes' return greatly to heart and had become more morose and bad-tempered. He refused to work, not only at the ashram but at the burning-ghāts, and he did not go back to his village but spent his time hanging round the smaller islands, lighting a fire on the shore of the fourth island, sleeping in the shelter of its one clump of trees, or landing where he chose to fish from the rocks of the last three dry and barren islets of the chain. Every evening his boat could be seen on the Sadhu's beach. If no other visitor was present, he and Prem would climb the steps to sit beside the holy man. It was then that this last attempt to move the ashram was planned and elaborated.

The idea from the first was Ram Kishen's. For some time the Sadhu would have none of it; it seemed too bold and outrageous to him and Ram Kishen's vindictiveness distressed him but, as the days went on and the self-satisfied busyness, the righteous bustle, on the next island became more difficult to ignore, he began to listen more attentively to what the Untouchable had to say.

Hari and Govind had both reported that the secretary was busy raising funds for the expansion of the ashram and school, with some success. There had been talk again of building on the bird island and even of a bridge. This was only a rumour in the air, but Prem brought the Sadhu positive information that the eagles had not yet settled on their nest. At his own insistence, his father had put him ashore early one morning under the giant tamarind and alone he had climbed to the rocky point above the eagles' tree and had lain there all day, watching the birds' uneasy coming and going. Soon it would be too late for them to breed that year, but the eagles could not bring themselves to leave the tree that they had known for so long. After listening to Prem, the Sadhu made up his mind.

This time the preparations were of the simplest. Nothing was needed beyond Ram Kishen's boat except a piece of sacking which he produced, having stolen it, although he did not tell the Sadhu this; there were also a coil of rope and a bottle of oil. Govind, when he was assured that it would be returned to him, provided the rope, which was thin and strong and supple, as the ropes of his nets were. He had no idea of the use to which it was to be put; perhaps he thought, if he thought at all, that the Sadhu had some private need of it. The oil was the same as that the holy man used for his body.

There was no point in delaying. Every day the danger of the ashram's population increasing became more likely. Soon the weather would change and the always unreliable mists would disappear altogether and the nights grow shorter. In warmer weather the island's sleepers would discard the wrappings with which they now covered their heads and leave their ears free to hear any sound. Pratap Singh, too, when the nights grew lighter and more temperate, would be inclined to leave the shelter of his hut and to make his patrols more frequently. Waiting only until the waning moon ceased to appear at all, the Sadhu, after some prayer and meditation, fixed a night for the attempt.

At first all went well, although that night there was no mist to help them and the stars shone brilliantly. Ram Kishen asked that when his boat left the Sadhu's island it should avoid the narrow channel and take the longer route round behind the ashram and then drift down in the shadow of the bird island, which lay beyond it, to land as far as possible from the temple. This meant a long paddle, but the Sadhu agreed. Prem, having refused to be left behind, was with them, but the holy man had insisted that he must stay in the boat and take no part in what was to be done. The readiness and meekness with which Prem agreed and Ram Kishen's silence should have warned the Sadhu, but his mind was busy with what lay before them.

The landing was made silently and uneventfully, and the boat secured in the black shadow of the rocks. At this point above them were only the steep side of the hill, a few of the remaining trees, and the bricks of the unfinished guesthouse. The Sadhu and Ram Kishen, who were naked except for their loin cloths, oiled the whole of their bodies carefully, as thieves do to enable them when surprised to slip out of any grasp. Prem gave them a cloth on which to dry their hands and passed them up the sacking and the rope, and they were ready to follow the by now well-worn path that led round the skirts of the island to the temple. The Sadhu did not know that Prem had left the boat and was following close behind them as invisibly and silently as any small, wild, nocturnal creature; he carried with him his pink shirt, newly washed and done up into a small packet.

They passed through the orchard and the cultivated plots of ground and now, at every step, their undertaking became more difficult. Although it was an hour past midnight, they were distressed to see, as they came closer to their goal, that not only was Pratap Singh's lantern burning by the jetty as they had expected but that there was a light in the top room of Dr. Mishra's house and a faint glow came from the temple itself. The Sadhu whispered to Ram Kishen to wait where he was, and advanced to reconnoitre the ground. As he disappeared into the darkness, Prem crept up and crouched beside his father. There was no need for them to whisper together; each knew exactly what they had privately planned to do.

The Sadhu flitted as silently as a bat through the starlit night. He made sure that the temple was empty and that the priests were sleeping soundly in their cells behind it. From the novices' quarters came the sound of heavy breathing, and of Pratap Singh there was no sign. It was impossible for him to see if Dr.

Mishra were awake or not, but the secretary was asleep on his cot with the black dispatch-box beside him in the downstairs room. The time was as favourable as it was likely to be. The Sadhu returned the way that he had come so silently that Prem would have been discovered if he had not glimpsed the holy man for a moment silhouetted against the stars in time to flatten himself on the ground behind his father. The two men, after another whispered consultation, crept towards the temple and the child followed them.

In the inner room the blue flame burning in its saucer of scented oil among the flowers on the altar showed the smiling face of the God. Ram Kishen hesitated, overcome by awe and fear, but the Sadhu advanced boldly into the sacred place and, putting out his hands, lifted the three-foot high image, holding it above the base. This was the crucial momet. They had no idea how heavy the God would be.

The image was made of wood carved and painted blue and decorated in green and gold by an artist whom the secretary, an acknowledged expert in such matters, had found and commissioned; it had cost Dr. Mishra a great deal of money, all of which had not gone to its maker. The God was not as heavy as they had feared. The Sadhu, with an effort, lifted the image from the low altar and, backing out of the inner place, turned and handed it to Ram Kishen. The Untouchable, using the great strength of his thick bowed legs, short back, and long arms, carried the image upright in his arms across the temple floor. The God, for the night, had been divested of most of his jewellery by the priests, but a necklace of gold beads which had been left, swung and tinkled as Ram Kishen moved. Prem, hiding behind a pillar, trembled anxiously.

Ram Kishen had forgotten the footprint enclosed by its gilded railing, and the Sadhu was just in time to prevent him from tripping over it. As they reached the edge of the temple floor and stepped cautiously down and out into the darkness, a priest called out loudly from the inner rooms. He was only calling in his sleep, but they did not know this and from that moment nothing went smoothly as they had planned.

Under the weight of the image in his arms, Ram Kishen could not move faster than a slow and stately walk and it was difficult for him to see where he was going. The Sadhu, fretting with impatience, guided him as well as he could down the path which led to the rock face below the Fakir's cave. At first there were steps to be climbed and buildings to skirt, and then the path became rough and stony and seldom used. The starlight exposed them to the night and it seemed impossible that they should not be seen and challenged and, as they passed the building which housed the sleeping monks and reached the rocks beyond it, they were seen, although they did not know it at the time and the one who saw did not believe what he had seen. A young novice, too lazy to climb the path to the latrines, had disobeyed Dr. Mishra's strict rule by creeping out to relieve himself among the rocks. Looking up, he glimpsed the bright image of the God, caught by the starlight as it swayed past high above him. Ram Kishen and the Sadhu heard him as he scurried away across the rocks to hide his fright in his bed-clothes and to decide that what he had seen was a dream. Later, of course, he was to say that he alone had seen the God in the course of his miraculous flight and to describe that shining passage. At the time, he caused Ram Kishen and the Sadhu much delay and embarrassment.

The sound of the novice's retreat brought Dr. Mishra, who was lying awake reading by the light of a candle, out on to his balcony. The old man, staring out into the darkness and seeing nothing, called loudly for Pratap Singh, and at once the whole island was astir.

The Sadhu and Ram Kishen lowered the image to the ground in the shadow of the rocks and crouched beside it. From the point which they had reached below the hill, they could see nothing of what was happening. They heard Pratap Singh's answering shout and the voices of the novices raised questioningly. It seemed to them that their theft must be discovered in a few moments. The Sadhu shook with silent laughter as he listened to the shouted questions and to the sleepy protesting voices of the priests, but Ram Kishen scowled anxiously into the darkness. He need not have worried. At the first alarm Prem darted forward and with one big breath blew out the small flame on the altar and, still holding his parcel carefully, hid himself behind a pillar and was now watching all that occurred, which was less than the listeners on the hill imagined.

A sleepy priest stood for a moment in the doorway at the back of the temple and seeing only that the lamp had gone out, probably from lack of oil, did not bother to light it again so soon before daybreak but called out that all was well, that nothing was there, as indeed nothing was, and went back to bed again. Pratap Singh, carrying his lantern and staff and grumbling loudly, set out to make the round of the island. The novices, one or two of whom had emerged from their building to gaze round them in the darkness, went back to their blankets. Only Dr. Mishra remained on his balcony silhouetted against the light in his room, waiting until the Sikh should complete his round. Prem, who had tiptoed out on to the terrace, saw him there and settled himself in the shadows where he could keep an eye on the old man, as well as on Pratap Singh's hut, while he waited for Ram Kishen's signal, an owl hooting twice, which he guessed would now be some time in coming.

Pratap Singh, on his way back towards the jetty, passed below the rocks where the Sadhu and Ram Kishen crouched beside the image. They saw the light of his lantern moving through the trees of the orchard and then heard him call up to Dr. Mishra that all was well. After waiting for some time to give the island a chance to settle down to sleep again, they resumed their journey, moving even more slowly and cautiously than they had done before. When they reached the foot of the iron ladder that led up to the cave, they lowered the image to the ground again and, carefully swathing it in the sacking, bound the rope firmly round it. The Sadhu went up the ladder first to make sure that the cave was ready to receive its visitor. Looking over his shoulder as he climbed, he saw that Pratap Singh's lantern was in its place before the hut and that there was now no light showing in Dr. Mishra's room. As he crawled into the cave, several bats swooped out, grazing his bare shoulders, but he was expecting them.

The Sadhu had never been in the cave before, having regarded it as the Fakir's property even after the old man was dead, and, as his eyes grew used to its darkness, he was surprised at its size beyond the funnel-shaped entrance; it was possible to stand upright and it went back several yards into the rock. As far as he could see there was no trace left of its former occupant and, making sure that nothing lurked in its darkness, he descended the ladder again. Ram Kishen, holding the rope, climbed up in his place and the most difficult and dangerous part of their undertaking began.

Ram Kishen hauled at the image from above and the Sadhu, climbing up behind it as it rose, guided it as best he could with one hand so that it should not scrape and bump on the rock face. Its progress seemed unduly slow to him. The hill was

visible from the jetty and the temple as well as from the islands
and the river and, in the starlight that shone directly on the
rock face, he felt as exposed as a fly on a wall. When at last the
base of the image disappeared over the edge of the opening
above him, he was tembling and covered with sweat. For a few
moments the two men lay side by side on the floor of the cave,
which was covered with mouse-like bat-droppings, to get
their breath. Then, to complete their plan, which was, in case
of the image's discovery, to make it seem that the God had
transported himself by his own volition to his new resting-
place, they removed the ropes and sacking and set the carved
and painted figure upright against the rock at the back of the
cave and smoothed away the marks left by their feet and bodies
in the dust and debris of the floor.

Ram Kishen could not see in the dark as the Sadhu could
and in the close blackness his fears returned. He backed away
from the image, whose gold ornaments, caught by the shaft of
starlight which came through the narrow entrance, gleamed
faintly at them from the darkness, and would have flung himself down the ladder if the Sadhu had not barred the way with
his own body. It was as well that he did so, for now, peering out,
he saw that someone was standing on the jetty holding the
lantern so that its light was reflected in the dark water.

It was Pratap Singh, who, knowing that his employer was
wakeful that night, was determined not to be caught napping

again by any fresh alarm. He was keeping himself awake by walking up and down the jetty and waving the lantern and by climbing up and down the path between the temple and Dr. Mishra's house. To the Sadhu's and Ram Kishen's dismay, it seemed as if he would continue this patrol all the rest of the night. Not daring to venture on to the ladder while the Sikh was about, they sat in the entrance of the cave, looking down, Ram Kishen fidgeting and cursing under his breath and the Sadhu preserving his calm with difficulty. Below them, Prem, waiting within a stone's throw of the jetty, was still more put out. Being so small and quick and dark, he was not afraid of being discovered, but he was growing sleepy and did not know how much longer he could stay awake. At last, as the Sadhu began to imagine that he could see the first signs of dawn in the sky, Pratap Singh put his lantern down in front of his hut and disappeared from view.

The Sadhu and Ram Kishen did not wait to see if he would reappear. Their two naked figures swung down the ladder one after the other in the starlight and vanished into the shadows between the rocks and the half-finished buildings that lay between them and their boat.

As they reached the orchard again, Ram Kishen, to prevent the holy man from discovering that Prem was not waiting for them, suddenly ran ahead down the path, as if overcome by panic, launched his boat and paddled off into the darkness before the other realized what he was doing. The Sadhu, standing on the strip of sand and staring after him in astonishment, heard the faint creak of a paddle and the sound of an owl calling twice on the night.

Dawn was near; although the darkness had not lessened, the Sadhu could feel it in the air. He could not stay where he was and there was only one thing to do. Wading out from the beach, he pushed off into the current, swimming strongly until he felt himself caught and swung and whirled away in the direction of his own island. A short struggle with the river ensued before the dark bulk of the rocks loomed up above him and he could seize and hang on to the trailing creepers and pull himself ashore.

As the Sadhu sat on the rocks in the already lessening darkness, wringing the water out of his long hair, he looked across at the other island where, although he did not know it, a brave but sleepy child had started up at the sound of the owl's call. Forgetting the pink shirt, which was left on the ground by the pillar, Prem had looked round to make sure that he was unobserved and had clambered up on to the broad, low shelf of the altar and, lying down among the flowers and resting his cheek on one hand, had fallen promptly asleep on the spot where the God had stood. The holy man, knowing nothing of this, felt pleased at the night's work. There had been anxious and awkward moments and Ram Kishen's behaviour at the

120

last had been inexplicable, but they had done what they had set out to do. The God had gone, as mysteriously and as suddenly as his footprint had appeared; this disappearance could only be interpreted as the withdrawing of his approval from the temple. Surely the work of the ashram could not continue round the mockery of an empty altar?

The Sadhu, unable to see across the water into the temple, sought his rock chamber and curling up beside the still smouldering embers of his fire slept peacefully until the sun rose.

Govind hurried up the steps and into the courtyard where the Sadhu, having finished his morning tasks, was feeding his flock of mynahs and sparrows. The fisherman was late with the day's provisions; the sun was already up above the trees and the holy man stood in a pool of sunshine, smiling to himself as he watched the birds. Govind began to talk excitedly as soon as he had climbed the steps, and the birds rose up together and flew away.

As the Sadhu listened, his face became expressionless. He seated himself cross-legged on the ground below the balustrade and motioned to Govind to do the same. The fisherman was too excited to keep still; he waved his arms, stood up and sat down again and scratched his old grey head as he talked. It was indeed a strange tale that he had to tell. .

The Brahmin priests in the first light had discovered that

the image of the God had vanished from the temple and that the son of Ram Kishen the Untouchable lay asleep on the altar in his place. Their cries of anger and dismay had brought everyone on the island running to the temple, including Pratap Singh, who had described the scene that followed to the fisherman.

It seemed that the child, woken from a deep sleep, had not wept or shown any surprise at his position, but, sitting up, had smiled and had begun to sing a sacred song. Dr. Mishra, so the Sikh had said, at first appeared to be too dazed or shocked to speak. The priests had wept and wrung their hands at this defilement of their temple and the novices, crowding in behind them, had added their voices to the tumult while the secretary, stepping forward, had snatched up the child and turned as if to put him roughly out of the temple, when he was stopped by Dr. Mishra, who, pulling the child away from him and lifting him in his arms, had begun to weep and cry out in a loud voice. When the others understood what he was saying, tumult had broken out again. According to Pratap Singh, the secretary had tried to take the child from the old man and the priests had become so threatening that he was forced to hurry to protect his employer, who continued to cry that the God's disappearance was a judgement on them all for forbidding Krishna's temple to anyone. At this point Govind himself had arrived with the day's supply of milk and, hearing the sound of shouts and angry voices, had tied his boat to the jetty and had rushed to the scene which, from now on, he could describe to the Sadhu at first hand.

The Sadhu, who during this recital had shut his eyes to hide the anger in them and was swaying his body backwards and forwards because, in his anxiety, he could not keep still, interrupted the old man to ask where Ram Kishen, the father of the child concerned, had been all the time. Govind refused to be hurried, and went on with the story in his own way.

The argument had continued on the terrace, where Dr. Mishra, still holding the child, faced the secretary and the angry priests. Only Govind, hovering on the edge of the crowd, had noticed that boats were approaching the island from two directions and converging on the jetty. The usual morning flotilla bringing the workmen from the direction of the town had arrived at the same time as the boat which held Ram Kishen and six of his fellow-villagers, wild-looking strong men armed with sticks and knives. Under the astonished gaze of the workmen, Ram Kishen had led his followers ashore, shouting that his child had been stolen away from his village in the night and uttering wild accusations against Dr. Mishra and the priests. The workmen had swarmed up the steps after him, eager to see what was happening, while the novices, being young and hot-headed, rushed forward to defend their temple. For a few moments the situation had looked ugly indeed, and Govind

123

had thought of making for his boat, but it was impossible for him to move against the crowd. Pratap Singh and the head mason between them had restored some kind of order while Dr. Mishra stepped forward with the child in his arms.

Prem, unruffled, had looked boldly back at the crowd with his sharp black eyes, but the old man who held him had wept bitterly. In the silence which followed the first sight of him, he told the assemblage, in a broken voice, of the God's disappearance and the discovery of the child left in his place. He said that he was heartbroken at Ram Kishen's accusations. This was no temple dedicated to Kali, the dark Goddess, but to Krishna, the Blessed Lord. He only wished his ashram and the island to be a happy place, and these continual excitements and alarms were wearing him out. Weeping again, he had motioned to Ram Kishen and his friends to enter the temple and declared that they were welcome there. At this the priests had protested, and the secretary, standing in front of Ram Kishen, had accused him roundly of the theft of the image and the substitution of the child.

For a few moments the crowd of workmen and boatmen, swayed by the secretary's vehemence, had been on his side, until Ram Kishen's followers, one and all, swore that he had passed the whole night in his village, talking and singing round the village fire until just before dawn, when he had gone to his hut and found that the child was missing. The secretary could not make them, by threats or by bribes, say otherwise and at last, disregarding him and escorted by as many as could squeeze into the small space, they had entered the temple with loud rejoicings.

At the sight of the empty altar confronting them, silence had fallen again, until the head mason cried out that he could not believe that the God had left them for good but that, in his mischievous fashion and as Mahabir Babu had said, to teach them all a lesson of love and humility, Krishna had hidden himself, perhaps somewhere close, and was waiting to be found.

The crowd instantly agreed with him and, leaving only Ram Kishen and his friends in the temple, had spread out over the island to search among the rocks and unfinished buildings. Govind had not gone with them. Trying to make himself inconspicuous, he had listened while the secretary tried to reason with Dr. Mishra.

It was impossible to move the stubborn and saintly old man from his decision, and presently the secretary, evidently making the best of what could not be helped or hoping, as Govind thought, that, if the image were found, its whereabouts might incriminate Ram Kishen, had joined in the search himself. It was he who, when no trace of the God had been discovered, suggested that a search should be made of the other islands and had ordered the boatmen to bring up the boats at once. Govind, not wishing his own boat, which was full of carefully piled nets, to be used, had slipped away to bring the news to the Sadhu. As he left, the boats loaded with men were already setting out for the island of the birds.

The Sadhu, when he heard this, jumped to his feet and with one swift movement vanished into the temple, leaving Govind to stare after him across the empty courtyard.

The old fisherman shook his head, grumbling to himself, and began to unpack the basket he had brought and to lay the fruit out under the thatched shelter below the swinging pots of plants. So much had happened already that morning to amaze him and to disarrange his old wits that he took the Sadhu's precipitate departure almost as a matter of course and when, after a few moments, the holy man reappeared beside him, breathing hard as if he had been running, he pretended not to notice and went on with what he was doing.

The Sadhu, when he ran out on to the rock ledges and looked across the water, saw first the cloud of disturbed birds which hovered above the trees and then the empty boats waiting on the sand below the tamarind. From where he stood he could hear sounds of crashing in the undergrowth and other sounds, a slashing and trampling, men's voices, loud shouts and calls. He saw the top of a tree shaking as if someone had climbed it to get a better view and then it seemed to him that across the water someone must be throwing stones into the trees; he distinctly heard the sound of stone on wood. He lifted his head and

126

looked into the sky. High above him the eagles, two minute specks, circled forlornly, seeming further away at every turn.

The Sadhu drew back into the trees. The search was over and the searchers, of whom he was dismayed to see at least twenty-five, were returning down the rock path and climbing into their boats. He glanced quickly across the channel at the ashram. A crowd still surrounded the temple and two distant figures stood beside the flagstaff on the hill, but there was no one on the iron ladder or at the mouth of the cave.

Suddenly he realized that the secretary's boat was making for his own island and, keeping out of sight among the rocks, the Sadhu ran back the way that he had come to the temple to receive his unwelcome visitors. Taking no notice of the old fisherman, he walked to the balustrade and seated himself above the river and, summoning his forces, waited for the boat to come in sight.

When the secretary, wearing his tightly buttoned grey coat and followed by the head mason and Pratap Singh, climbed the steps and, after shuffling off his shoes, passed into the courtyard, the first thing that he saw was the Sadhu's dark, still shape against the brightness of the river. The holy man sat cross-legged and straight-backed on the balustrade, with his hands resting on his thighs. The sunny courtyard was full of the chirping of birds and the scent of flowers. For a few moments the secretary hesitated; it even occurred to him that he might go quietly away without speaking to anyone, after perhaps resting for a short while on the warm ground under the trees. Then he pulled himself together and, crossing the courtyard, asked the holy man politely if he might make a brief search of the island. Glancing at Govind, he added that undoubtedly the Sadhu had already heard the news and understood what he was looking for.

The Sadhu raised his hand in a dignified gesture of assent. Pratap Singh cried out that he would take no part in the search, which was an insult to the holy man, but that he would wait where he was. The secretary, smiling scornfully and straightening his horn-rimmed spectacles, marched across the courtyard and into the temple, followed by the head mason.

They were gone only a short time. The ruins and the small, bare rooms of the temple were easily seen and the maze of sandy paths beyond all led out on to the same rock ledges. This island was smaller than the secretary had thought and seemed to have no secrets. He had seen no sign of life, nothing except the sunny rocks, a view of the other islands and a few trees, but when he returned to the courtyard he was suspicious and angry. Standing in front of the Sadhu, who had not altered his position, he said loudly that, the age of miracles being past, he was certain that an elaborate hoax had been played on the ashram, that the image had been removed by human agency and hidden somewhere not far off, and that he meant to find it even if he had to tear all seven islands apart, especially the one they had already visited that morning where the thick jungle had not yet been properly searched.

The Sadhu sighed and stretched himself and looked around him, as if he were coming out of a trance. His voice was gentle and sweet after the loud, harsh tone used by the Bengali. What a pity it was, he said, apparently to Pratap Singh waiting by the steps, that no one had thought of asking him if he knew where the God, undoubtedly with good reason, had chosen to hide his likeness from them. Was it not generally known that holy men had at times the power to see what other men could not see? Let there be no more disturbance, noise, or trouble. Let them all go away and leave him and his island in peace. If they looked, where they might have thought of looking before, they would see what he had just seen quite plainly: an image, which could only be that of Krishna, shining blue and green and gold in the darkness of the old Fakir's cave.

No one spoke. The secretary stared at the serene face before him, then turned and walked out of the courtyard and down the steps. The head mason and Govind each made a hurried obeisance and ran after him, the fisherman forgetting his basket in his excitement. Pratap Singh, after a long look at the Sadhu, who had shut his eyes again and resumed his pose, followed them more slowly.

The Sadhu sat where he was long after the creaking of oars and the sound of excited voices had died away. There was nothing about his still figure and bent head to disturb the birds and presently they flew down from the trees and began to pick up the scattered grain.

When the last grain had gone and the courtyard was empty, the Sadhu stood up and, walking into the sunshine of the open space, threw himself on to the ground before the temple and in shame and repentance put dust on his head.

5

All that day the eagles circled over the islands, calling their harsh, sad cries. Towards evening, they planed down together to the river, spilling the air from their wings, and wheeled close over the rocks where the Sadhu stood waiting for them.

He had known that they would go before sunset, and now, once more, he called them to him with their own cry. For the last time they came, sailing close in past his head, wheeling and turning above the trees and the roof of his temple, their pale heads, with the fierce yellow eyes and cruel beaks, turned to look down at him. He lifted his arms towards them in farewell and watched them circle up and up, away from him and out of sight. When the sky was empty, he went back to the temple where evening had come. Entering the cramped cell above the river, he blocked the narrow entrance behind him with stones, which he had put ready for that purpose, and began the long fast and meditation, the penance which he needed to undergo.

6

For two weeks the Sadhu did not leave his cell. He crouched against the rough stone of its walls, breathing its cold musty air, unable to stand upright or to lie down, or to move more than a few feet in any direction. In the first four days he did not permit himself to put his eye to the narrow aperture that looked towards the river which ran below him, nor did he eat or drink.

It had been many years since he had undergone this discipline. He had thought himself beyond the need of it. During these four days he pondered on his actions of the last months, on his obstinacy, self-will, and his concern to alter the course of things, whose course is God's. On the fifth day he removed a stone from the entrance of the cell and, putting his hand out, groped for the pitcher of water which he knew that he would find there. Before making his retreat he had left a sign on the earth of the courtyard that Govind would understand.

In the past, when the Sadhu had often disappeared from the world in this manner and there had been no disciple on the island at the time, it had been the fisherman's privilege to see that the pitcher of water was freshly filled and to supplement it on the seventh day, if the holy man had not emerged by then, with a small quantity of curds. After he had drunk a few mouthfuls of water, the Sadhu replaced the stone and looked through his narrow loophole out over the river where the sun was setting. At this time every day the cell was filled with a strong gold light, that persisted for a short time. When it had gone and darkness had closed in once more, he shut his eyes and leaned his head against the stone. Now he was no longer concerned with himself or with the world beyond the cell. He felt no pain or cold, hunger or thirst. He was free, light and clear and unimpeded. The way of bliss was open to him once more, and now the rock walls held only the small, quiet, scarcely breathing shell of his body. He returned to that body during the next nine days only for short intervals.

In these two weeks the island had several visitors besides Govind, who every morning swept the courtyard and watered the Sadhu's plants, scattered the grain for the birds and set two saucers of milk on the ground behind the temple, for it was not the Sadhu's intention that the island's creatures should do penance with him by going without these small indulgences. Hari came three or four times in his boat and grew more annoyed at each visit to find the Sadhu still absent. He missed the afternoon discussions and he also wanted to hear what the holy man had to say about the theft of the image and to give him the latest news of the ashram, where Dr. Mishra had quarrelled with his secretary, who nevertheless refused to leave his employment or the island. The old man, everyone agreed, was becoming rather peculiar; he had insisted that the image of Krishna should stay where it was in the cave and that the cave should become another temple. This was causing great inconvenience to the priests and novices, who disliked the climb up the iron ladder. In the temple by the jetty the altar was still bare.

Ram Kishen had made no attempt to see the Sadhu for several days after their adventure. He knew very well that the holy man was displeased with him, and he kept away for as long as he could. When he and Prem at last came to the island in the late afternoon of the sixth day of the Sadhu's retreat and climbed the steps, it was to say good-bye. Now that he had gained the right of entry to the temple, Ram Kishen had no desire to worship there; there were other temples in the land where he would be forbidden to put his foot. He was still defiant and restless and, although he was not afraid of the secretary's suspicions, he thought that it would perhaps be wise for him to disappear from the neighbourhood for some time. He put his belongings and his son into his boat and set off to look for work at the railway junction and ferry fifty miles downstream, pausing only at the island on his way.

There was no familiar figure waiting for them on the steps and the courtyard was empty. Prem ran ahead through the temple rooms calling shrilly for his friend. The child was wearing his pink shirt and carried a bunch of flowers as a farewell present. When Ram Kishen, following more slowly, saw that the entrance to the cell was blocked, he knew that there was no

point in delaying their journey any longer. Prem could not believe that he was not to see the Sadhu and, when his father took
his hand to lead him away, he began to cry and to struggle and
Ram Kishen had to take him up in his arms to prevent him from
beating on the stone. If the Sadhu heard them, he gave no sign
and, laying the offering of flowers on the steps, Ram Kishen
carried the weeping Prem back to the boat.

One morning, soon after Govind had finished his chores and
rowed off, the secretary came alone to the island. He could not
have said why he had taken the trouble to row himself across
from the ashram but he, too, was disappointed to find the
courtyard and temple empty. He knew nothing of the cell behind the stones, but he felt that the Sadhu was somewhere
about, and he waited in the courtyard, sitting on the balustrade
where the Sadhu had sat. He looked, as he always did, self-
contained, neat, and inconspicuous in his grey coat and white
dhotie. His glasses hid his eyes and his rather flat, yellow-brown,
smooth face was expressionless; there was nothing to show what
was on his mind. After sitting for some time with his hands in
his lap, staring at the ground, he sighed and went away.

It was dawn on the fourteenth day when the Sadhu emerged
from his cell. He walked very slowly across the temple and leant
for a moment against the doorpost. The world was full of a grey
light which hurt his eyes and from the trees of the courtyard
came the first bird notes. Moving slowly and weakly, he

crossed the courtyard and crept down the steps to the river and lowered his shrunken, dry, and grimy body and dust-matted hair into the water until it covered him completely. For a long time he lay in the river with only his nostrils above the surface, feeling life coming back into him. Then he turned over and, kicking out feebly, swam a few strokes. He stood on the beach again, scrubbing his body with sand, stretching his muscles, wringing water out of his hair. After another immersion in the healing river, a long drink, and the chanting of a prayer, he was able to climb the steps to find the pot of curds and the small handful of grain which he needed to give him strength for what he had to do before it was time for Govind to arrive. This was to reach the hidden bay among the rocks of the shore line and to push his boat out into the stream where the current would catch it and whirl it away out of his sight and mind.

When the Sadhu returned, the sun was rising dazzlingly. He stood on the rocks where its rays would fall directly on him and combed and oiled his long hair. Below him the river took on its clean, morning colours and the islands swam in the fresh, pure light. Over the rocks was the summit of the hill above the ashram and, when he turned his head, he could see the green tops of the trees on the bird island and beyond it the curving end of the chain. He knew, calmly and without sorrow, that he would never climb the rock path behind the leaves again and never enter the glade below the great fluted stone, or look down on the tree where once the eagles had nested. In the long hours of meditation he had seen the full circle of his actions. Now he had done with meddling and had ceased to concern himself with what must be. The fate of the island and its bird inhabitants he had laid in the hand of God.

As he wandered back to the temple, he began to sing a loud and joyful song and from the trees his flock of mynahs and sparrows rose into the air and followed him.

When Govind arrived with his basket, the Sadhu was sweeping out the courtyard as he had always done. The old man went to him and, kneeling down, humbly touched his feet.

Part Three

I

꧁꧁꧁꧁꧁ A month went by, each day longer than the last and each night clearer and more brilliant. The river ran sluggishly in its channels and new sandbanks appeared. The air was full of fine drifting sand and the distant hills retreated in the haze until they could no longer be seen. On the islands the trees, which had been bare or covered with dry and dusty leaves, suddenly put on a new and vivid green. → This is fevarish too

Work on the ashram contined almost feverishly. Buildings were finished and new buildings begun. The ashram's fame grew as the tales of the extraordinary events that had occurred on the island spread further through the countryside. The number of

novices in residence increased and boats plied back and forth
between the island and the mainland, bringing curious visitors.
A compromise between Dr. Mishra, the secretary, and the priests
had been reached. In the temple by the jetty, which was seldom
empty, new images had been enthroned: Krishna and Radha,
his beloved, seated side by side, but at any time of the day a
figure, usually that of a priest or a novice, could be seen climbing
the ladder to the cave. The island hummed with busy life. Blue
clouds of incense rose into the air and the hammering and
shouting of the workmen and the sounds of chanting, of bells,
and of conches, reached to the other islands.

The Sadhu let none of this disturb him. He went about his
daily tasks, fed his birds, played with his squirrel, performed his
ritual, received his few visitors and passed his nights in his rock
chamber with his silent companions. Hari, who spent his spare
time on the islands, found him a little remote in his manner,
but the sense of peace and well-being he gave to those near him
was intensified.

As for the bird island, it lay behind its screen of leaves,
waiting for what was to come.

One hot and oppressive afternoon, the glade below the great
stone was a pool of sunshine. The trees stood round it like
sentinels. The leaves hung limply, and in the drowsy warmth
the scent of grass and of flowers, mingling with the island's
pervading stench of old bird-droppings, was stronger than

usual and the insect sounds, the low whirring and humming that came from the sun-drenched bushes were strangely loud. A sunbird disturbed this unnatural stillness as it flitted from bush to bush. Its long, curved beak explored the flowers. The leaves swayed as it hung from them and, freed of its minute weight, lifted again, leaving a ripple of movement in its wake. Its yellow breast shone as it twisted and turned through the leaves, and the sunlight gave its purple back a metallic sheen. As it moved through the bushes, the silence was broken by its light, tinkling call. Alarmed perhaps by the shadow that was now creeping over the glade, the bird suddenly flew up and across the huge rock face behind it to perch for a few seconds on the summit of the stone, turning its head searchingly and moving its wings. The shadow reached the stone and a dark and ominous cloud rose up behind the trees. A low rumble of distant thunder sounded through the glade.

The Sadhu, on his island, climbed the rocks to watch the flashes of lightning as the ridge of angry purple cloud mounted up the sky. He had weathered many such storms before and was not alarmed, but he went unhurriedly back to the courtyard and moved his hanging pots and baskets of plants into an inner room and closed the temple's thick old doors with a strong bar and socket.

On the next island, the workmen made for the boats and were rowed hastily to the mainland while the permanent inhabitants of the ashram looked apprehensively at the advancing clouds and made the buildings as secure as possible. There was a great deal of running about and shouting, but there was little that anyone could do except to close the shutters over the windows of Dr. Mishra's house and the novices' quarters.

The fishing-boats on the river hauled in their nets and scurried for the shore; the sudden and violent nor'westers which appeared without warning at that time of the year were not to be trifled with. The sky darkened and the light changed and became yellowish and dull. The river was the colour of lead and on the islands the rocks turned a livid tone. Flocks of egrets flew hurriedly back to the shelter of the bird island and in the three heronries there was a heavy rustling and stirring, a crackling of twigs, and the sound of large wings opening and folding, as the birds moved to the lower branches and the sheltered side of their trees. All over the islands there was a scurrying, quick movement, chirps and rustlings and cries of alarm as every living thing sought the nearest hole and shelter. In the pause that followed, there was an ominous waiting stillness and silence which spread across the water to the mainland.

The wind came first, and with it the sand. The river was lashed into abrupt, white-topped waves and the driving clouds of sand, caught up and carried far inland, blotted out the islands below. Heavy rain followed close on the sandstorm and thunder pealed and rolled above the river. The storm, compact and dark, advanced on a narrow front across the river as if directed towards the seven islands by an invisible finger; it could not hurt the barren rocks but on the fourth island it tore the leaves from the clump of trees and heaped the stones with sand; its fringe passed over the bird island where the trees bent and groaned, their lamentations lost in the huge voice of the wind; it touched the Sadhu's island, carrying away the thatched shelter and the hut where once his disciples had lived; but the fury of the storm and the force of its dark core was hurled against the island of the ashram. There the wind shrieked vindictively in many voices and in the twilight vague shapes swayed and whirled. The air was thick with flying, stinging sand, bricks, branches, sheets of corrugated iron, until the rain descended, drowning even the wind.

The storm soon passed, as such storms do. The air lightened and the wind began to lessen. The curtain of rain withdrew from the islands and swept on towards the mainland. The clouds vanished with the wind, and in a surprisingly short time the sun shone again. The islands, streaming with moisture, shook themselves and took stock of the damage.

On the bird island the only casualties were a few nests and the eagles' tree, which had withstood many storms. The deserted nest had gone first and the fishy debris of years, the old fish scales and bones and dry droppings and feathers, sticks and straws had been whirled up and scattered far over the island.

Then the wind had stripped the tree of its leaves and, unable to uproot it from its deep hold between the rocks, had snapped its trunk a few feet from the ground and had dropped it into the river, which carried it away.

The Sadhu, too, had been let off lightly. While the sand-storm lasted he had crouched in the temple, but as the rain fell he had slipped out of the rear entrance and had watched the progress of the storm, clinging to the rocks to prevent himself from being carried away by the wind, his hair almost torn from his head and his body lashed by the rain. He had shouted and sung with pleasure and excitement as he faced the river. When the storm was over, he had descended to the courtyard, where the bamboo poles of the shelter still stood against the temple wall; the loss of the disciples' hut, as it was no longer of any use, had not distressed him. A few branches had gone from his tree and his island was covered with a debris of leaves and sticks, and spume and refuse from the river. Before ascending to his rock for his evening prayers, the Sadhu set about the tidy-ing of his island, putting it in good order again.

The ashram had received the full force of the storm which, so great was the damage, might have been directed only against it. The secretary, clutching the black tin dispatch-box, had fled, with the novices and a priest, Pratap Singh, and other hangers-on of the ashram, from the fury of the wind when the first roof was torn away, to shelter as best they could among the rocks on the steep leeward side of the island. Dr. Mishra and the second priest had been in the cave when the storm struck, and there they had stayed, soaked by the rain driving through the narrow entrance but safe and less uncomfortable than the others.

When the storm passed and they all crept back to view the scene, they found that not one building was still standing. The corrugated-iron roofs had been plucked away as if by a giant hand and the walls levelled. On the hill the flagstaff had been snapped off and the flag torn to shreds. Pratap Singh's hut and the bamboo jetty had disappeared as if they had never been. The pillars of the temple still stood, but the images of Krishna and Radha had been torn from the altar on a great gust of wind and whirled away by the river. Of the ashram, nothing remained but an untidy rubble of brick and the original image of Krishna safe in the old Fakir's cave.

2

On the evening after the storm, when the Sadhu descended from his rock perch and, in the growing darkness, returned to the temple, he knew that the ashram had gone. His old powers had come back to him, and he did not need to go early next morning to the rock ledges to see the destruction across the water. He went about his tasks quietly in the courtyard until Govind arrived, bringing the news, and then he listened courteously, without comment, to the excited old fisherman's story.

The rest of the day the Sadhu spent in and about the temple, sweeping away blown sand and leaves, giving each room a good spring cleaning, washing down the uneven floors, brushing cobwebs from the cracked ceilings. He put fresh flowers on the altar stone and in the niches of the shrine: roses from his two bushes, hibiscus and oleander from the island's bushes that had escaped the storm and were just coming into bloom. When all was ready, he went down to the river and bathed himself and washed his hair and his piece of red silk, which he spread out on the balustrade to dry. He knew that he would have no visitors that afternoon and at midday, after he had fed his birds and filled the saucers with milk for the snakes, he knelt in front of the flat altar stone, resting his weight on his heels and holding his hands on his lap. There he stayed without moving until it grew dark.

148

The next afternoon, with his striped squirrel on his shoulder, he was ready and waiting in his usual place at the top of the steps to receive Hari when he came.

The merchant, who now wore a thin coat of cream-coloured poplin and carried a palm-leaf fan in one hand, climbed the steps heavily, leaning on his cane, while behind him his two boatmen, having folded his umbrella and laid it back in the boat, sat together on the beach, smoking biris, the brown country cigarettes. Hari was sweating after the long row in the afternoon heat, and sitting down beside the Sadhu, he fanned himself for a few moments in silence. The river, a colourless flood under a colourless sky, ran past the island with its soothing murmuring sound, and the shadows of the leaves above them might have been painted on the stone.

When Hari spoke, he did not at first mention the storm or the ashram, but asked abruptly if the holy man had heard anything of Ram Kishen the Untouchable and his child. The Sadhu, surprised, shook his head, and after a pause said that he only knew that they were a long way off, perhaps hundreds of miles. He added, more to himself than to Hari, that Ram Kishen and Prem would not return to the island or to their village for many years.

The merchant sighed deeply and said that the Sadhu, if he knew this, knew, of course, what had happened much nearer at hand and there was no need to comment on the storm or to describe the state of the ashram and the ruins of its temple. But could the holy man, in his wisdom, explain to him why the storm should have spared not only the mainland lying directly in its path but six out of the seven islands, only to fall with such fury on the ashram? It seemed, after the happenings of the last months, as if the Gods were playing a strange game with the ashram and poor old Mishra, a game of cat and mouse. He, himself, did not know what to think.

The Sadhu frowned and then smiled at his friend's fat, shrewd, but troubled face. He put his hand on Hari's knee and, after a moment, told him gently to clear his mind of its confused and troubled thoughts. He could promise him that Dr. Mishra would before long be more content and at peace than he had ever been. As for Ram Kishen and his son, they were only what they seemed, an unfortunate and poor man and a small and innocent child. He himself, as the merchant very well knew, was a simple religious and had no powers over the heavens or the winds. The destruction of the ashram was the will of God.

Hari sighed again, shaking his head sadly. But why, he asked, looking up at the Sadhu, why should the Gods wish to destroy such a holy undertaking and to humble a good and saintly old man? What could be the reason? The ways of the Gods were indeed past understanding. He, Hari, would do better to give up his search and to concern himself only with his ledgers and bank account.

For a moment the Sadhu did not answer. He was watching a flight of egrets, each bird as white as foam, pass across the sky on their way back to their island home where they would sink into their chosen tree and fold their wings and settle on their long legs for the night. When he turned back to the merchant, his smile was still sweet but also a little sly and mocking, and in his eyes, which he kept veiled by his long lashes, was a look that would have seemed wild and disturbing to Hari. Gently he agreed that the ways of God were hard for human understanding, but that, somewhere, there was always a reason.

For an hour or two they sat together, talking a little, but often silent, while the sun sank lower in the sky and from the river came the cool breath of evening. Presently Hari rose and took his leave and went away, soothed and comforted.

3

The whole neighbourhood was shocked by the news of the destruction of the ashram. Boats put out and circled the island to view the damage and there was much sympathy for Dr. Mishra. Only he, a priest, five novices, and, at night, the faithful Pratap Singh were able to stay on, existing very uncomfortably among the ruins. The rest of the community had found temporary shelter on the mainland, where the storm had done little damage; a few fishermen had lost their nets, a tree or two had fallen, roofs had lost their tiles or thatch. The secretary, on the second day after the storm, had left the island, taking the dispatch-box of papers and ledgers with him, for Benares, where, it was rumoured, he was to sell securities and to raise funds on Dr. Mishra's behalf for the rebuilding of the temple and eventually of the other buildings.

When, two weeks later, he had not come back, a fresh crop of rumours began to circulate. It was first hinted and then openly said that the concrete which had been used in the construction of the buildings was of very poor quality, being mainly sand. The head mason denied this hotly, and Hari Das Thirani, who had supplied some of the cement and knew that there was nothing wrong with it, was indignant. Nothing could be proved but, when the days went by and there was no sign of the secretary, this rumour at least was accepted as fact.

No one except Dr. Mishra was surprised when it became known that the secretary had decamped, taking with him all that was left of the ashram's funds and Dr. Mishra's fortune. The old man refused to believe this villainy and continued to assert that he trusted his secretary as he did himself. It was not until definite proof was sent to him from Benares that he gave in and accepted the fact that he had nothing left. Many of the wealthy men of the district had lost money too. Public opinion stiffened and the caste Hindus began to say that this was a judgement on him for opening the temple to those who should never have entered it.

Dr. Mishra had hoped that he would be able to build a few new humble buildings, made perhaps of dried mud, bamboo, and thatch, to replace the rough shelters in which his faithful ones were now living. He talked enthusiastically of the virtue of the simple life and of the aesthetic advantages of such structures over brick and concrete, and even argued that perhaps he had been too presumptuous in his ideas before. When Hari, who liked and pitied the old man but did not wish to offend his fellow merchants and neighbours, broke it to him as gently as possible that there was no hope of raising any fresh funds at all, the shock was too much. Dr. Mishra was a gentle, sweet, and courteous as he had always been, but it was soon seen by those near him that his wits were astray.

Pratap Singh, who had not been paid his wages for some time, was the first to leave when he went regretfully to look for other work. Before long, his licence having been restored, he was driving his taxi again, to the danger of everyone in the town. One by one the others slipped away, until there was only one young novice left on the island with Dr. Mishra.

The two moved into the orchard. The hot weather had come and they were grateful for the shade of the few trees which the workmen and the storm had spared. There they lived in a small thatched hut which Hari had secretly caused to be made for them, not far from the plot of cultivated ground and the rocks where the Sadhu had grounded his boat in the shadow of the hibiscus bush on the night of his first adventure on the island. Govind, in his boat, brought them milk and fruit and the few provisions they needed, which at first were also supplied by Hari but later by the villagers, who regarded Dr. Mishra as a saint.

The old man and his disciple kept the cave, which they considered their temple, clean and tidy. They put what flowers they could find before the image of Krishna, and offered pujah there on the appropriate days. Hari, who on his way back from visiting the Sadhu would sometimes call at the island, although he never climbed the ladder to the cave, reported that the old man was content and even happy. Fishermen from their boats would see the blue smoke of his fire rising above the orchard trees, or see him, still agile and active, climbing the iron ladder, or wandering about the rocks of the island, waving his arms and talking and singing to himself, naked except for his sacred thread and the muslin dhotie which he still wore, his white hair, long now, moving in the breeze. Before the hot weather was over and the rains came, the young novice, too, went away and Dr. Mishra, who did not notice that the boy had gone, was left alone.

4

ॐ The years went by and the seven islands were forgotten except by a few. Round them the life of the river went on as it had always done. The country-boats passed with spread sails. A river steamer made its way upstream. Fishermen cast their nets, the water birds waded in the shallows. Porpoises turned and played. The wild duck, like the seasons, came and went. The stories told of the islands in the villages of the mainland changed into legends. Although they were known to be extremely holy ground, very few people came near them and only the Sadhu's island was still visited; the others were avoided and if a stranger, who had taken the trouble to have himself rowed out from the town, wished to explore behind the screen of trees on the bird island, he was put off by his boatmen with vague excuses. Fishermen in their boats, passing close to the island where now the ruins of the ashram were hidden by a thick pall of green and the trees flourished again, declared that in the evenings they would hear the sweet, high notes of a flute sounding from the hills, the rocks, and the trees, although there was no one to be seen except the white-haired old man seated at the threshold of his hut, and they all knew him, as they knew the Sadhu on his rock perch.

Often the Sadhu, in his wanderings about his island, would

look across the channel that divided them and see Dr. Mishra seated there, cross-legged before his hut in the shade of his orchard trees. Sometimes the Sadhu would sit down himself on the rocks and the two would contemplate each other across the water. This remote companionship satisfied them and they did not show by sign or gesture that they were aware of each other.

Although the Sadhu always watched for them through the years and standing on the rocks at the centre of his island would often search the skies and call their own cry up into the blue, the eagles never came back.

A NOTE ON THE TYPE

The text of this book was set on the Linotype in Fairfield, the first type-face from the hand of the distinguished American artist and engraver Rudolph Ruzicka. In its structure Fairfield displays the sober and sane qualities of a master craftsman whose talent has long been dedicated to clarity.

Rudolph Ruzicka was born in Bohemia in 1883 and came to America in 1894. He has designed and illustrated many books and has created a considerable list of individual prints—wood-engravings, line-engravings on copper, aquatints.

The book was composed, printed, and bound by H. Wolff, New York. The paper was made by S. D. Warren Co., Boston, Mass. Typography and binding design by George Salter.